SOME CALL IT TEMPTATION

A SWEET DREAMS NOVEL

SARAH PEIS

Some Call It Temptation
© 2019 Sarah Peis
Published by Hexatorial
Developmental Editing: Natasha Orme
Copy Editing: Hot Tree Editing
Cover Art: Tall Story Design
ISBN ebook 978-0-6481085-3-5
ISBN print 978-0-6481085-5-9

All rights reserved. No part of this book may be reproduced, scanned, or distributed in any manner whatsoever without written permission from the author. This is a work of fiction. Names, characters, businesses, places, events and incidents are either the products of the author's wild imagination or used in a fictitious manner. Any resemblance to actual persons, living or dead, or actual events is purely coincidental. Except for Willa's love for cupcakes. That's based on a real person. Me.

DEDICATION

To Andouillette. May we never meet again.

1

"That's not the right hole. You have to stick it in here."

"I know where to put it in. Go away and let the professionals do their jobs."

"And I'm not a professional?"

"Not when you wave that thing at me. It stinks."

I watched Landon, one of the mechanics, and Mason, one of the owners of Drake's Garage, argue from where I was standing in the doorway. Their heads were under the hood of an old car that looked ready to go to the junkyard, and they were bickering while Landon was eating a giant sandwich.

I worked at Drake's while their receptionist Willa was traveling around Europe with her boyfriend, Jameson, the other owner of the garage and Mason's brother. Willa was one of my best friends, and when she found out that I didn't have a job lined up after I finished college, she asked if I could help out while she was away.

Since I needed the money and there wasn't anything I wouldn't do for her, I agreed. I was desperate to get out of my hometown, Humptulips, and to be able to do that, I needed to save up some money. The small, sleepy town was in the middle of nowhere, and if I wanted to get out from under my mother's thumb, my only option was to move away. Not only had Willa organized a job for me, she also let me stay at her apartment rent free for as long as I needed.

When they stopped arguing to take breaths, I seized the opportunity to call out to them, "Carter is on the phone. He wants to speak to Mason."

I heard a loud groan, followed by a bang, and then Mason's head came up from underneath the hood.

"Can't you handle it?" he muttered. "I'm never doing a favor for Willa again."

There went my hard-won equilibrium. "You're doing *her* a favor? Don't you mean I'm doing *you* a favor by helping out while she's travelling?"

He brushed me off and went inside the office. "We could have hired someone from the temp agency."

I followed him and stood on the opposite side of the desk. It was always a good idea to put space between me and Mason. Things happened when we were standing too close. Confusing things.

"You mean the temp agency that blocked your number?"

He grumbled something unintelligible under his breath and picked up the receiver. After talking to Carter for all of five seconds, he hung up, then aimed another glare at me and stalked out.

I rolled my eyes at the closed door and got back to work. His annoyance at my presence wasn't anything new. And I'd learned to just ignore it. For the most part.

The day was busy, the garage popular, and I lost track of time. I was entering numbers into a spreadsheet when I felt someone watching me. Judging by the raised hairs on my arm and the warmth I felt in my belly, it could only be one person.

"Is there a reason why you're back already?" I asked, my voice sugary sweet. No point poking the bear unnecessarily.

"I need more oil filters for the Bronco," Mason said, his stare game going strong today.

I nodded. "Okay."

"Why aren't you writing this down?" he asked, the deep timbre of his voice resonating through my body.

"Because I'll be able to remember oil filters."

Despite what he thought, I wasn't an idiot. But try telling him that. He seemed to have cast his judgment already.

"I also need brake pads for the Mustang."

I forced a smile on my face. "No problem. Anything else?"

"Spark plugs for the Audi."

"You got it."

"You're still not writing anything down. How do you know how many to order for each?"

I fought the eye roll and won. "That's three items. And Willa wrote down how many to order of each before she left. I think I can remember three things." I sighed.

"Can you, though?"

I ignored his jab and smiled at him sweetly. I had perfected putting a mask in place when I needed to, and good manners had been drilled into me from birth. "Anything else?"

"I need it by tomorrow."

"No problem."

"Means you need to send the order now."

Not sure how much longer I could hold back that eye

roll that was desperate to come out. "I can handle it. Now can I get back to work?"

He didn't say anything else, just glared at me with his beautiful emerald eyes—that were totally wasted on the jerky shithead—and left the office. Good riddance. There was only so much time someone could spend staring at all the gloriousness that was Mason Drake. Too bad he was such a butt wipe.

One that had the nicest arms I had ever seen. They were muscular and defined. And I've always had a weakness for toned arms. They were my kryptonite. Fortunately, he didn't know that. Unfortunately, he liked to wear tight T-shirts that showed me entirely too much.

I made myself another cup of instant coffee—the only thing available since I broke the coffee machine on my second day at the office—and ordered the parts His Majesty requested.

The day went by in a blur, and I was still in the office an hour after closing. Willa told me I could leave as soon as I turned the Closed sign on the door. Technically that was true. But since the computer wasn't working properly, everything took forever, and I had a few invoices I needed to pay.

Tonight was one of the nights I usually babysat for my friend Nora, and I only had thirty minutes to get home. Lucky for me, peak-hour traffic wasn't a thing in Humptulips. I would have time to finish answering the last email that was titled urgent, then could rush home and still make it.

The workshop was busy, and the guys usually worked long hours, so there were still plenty of people around.

Landon came inside as I was packing up. "What are you still doing here?" he asked and stopped at the door with his brows raised.

"I'm on my way out, just had to finish up a few things."

"Pretty much anything can wait until tomorrow. You don't have to work late, you know."

I liked to do a good job and that meant getting my work done. Despite what most people thought about me, I was not a ditzy idiot. I got a scholarship to college and I studied hard.

None of the things I accomplished in my life were because of who my family was. The Connors were notorious in Humptulips; my mother owned a huge cattle ranch and half the businesses in town. Everyone thought I had it all, but nobody really knew how oppressive a life I had led.

I shouldered my bag and gave him a half-smile, which was all I had in me at the moment. "Didn't want to mess up on my first day. The computer wasn't working properly, so it took a bit longer. But I got it done."

He nodded and walked closer. "If you ever need anything, come and find me."

I guessed him to be around my age, and he had the boy-next-door look perfected. His light green eyes and curly dark brown hair would make many a woman sigh in delight. Something I knew for a fact since I'd seen him in action.

I made my way to the door. "Thanks, that's a really nice offer. I will."

The door to the garage opened again and Mason stepped inside, sucking all the air from the room. I guessed his big head needed the extra oxygen to function.

"What's a nice offer?" he asked.

I rolled my eyes at his gruff voice and kept walking. "Nothing. I'll see you tomorrow."

He didn't respond, but judging by his narrowed eyes,

he wasn't all that happy. But then again, I didn't think I had ever seen him so much as smile at me. He was happy-go-lucky with everyone else, but as soon as he saw me he went all frostbite.

He'd been around when I visited Willa at work before, and we've all gone out together a few times. He was hard to avoid; his brother was dating my best friend, yet for some reason, we always seemed to disagree about something.

I ignored his angry scowl and waved goodbye to Landon. I really had to hurry up, or Nora would think I wasn't gonna show.

The drive home was blissfully uneventful, and I made it with a few minutes to spare. I dropped all my stuff into Willa's apartment before going next door.

I opened the door with the key Nora had given me and was greeted by her three-year-old boy, Luca. "Esteballa, you are here," he yelled while dancing toward me wearing only his underwear and dinosaur slippers. I loved that he had a special name for me and secretly hoped he'd never be able to say my name properly.

Nora was a single mom who had been dealt a few blows in life, but she never let anything keep her down. I did what I could to help, especially since she had no support from her family or the kids' dad and was raising them by herself.

We met when I first moved in with Willa. I was heading out to meet Maisie and ran into Nora, who was struggling up the stairs with two kids and a bag of groceries. I gave her a hand and we bonded over our mutual love of unpronounceable cheese.

"Hey, bud, how was your day?" I asked.

"I gots to play with Pete t'day."

I kissed his chubby cheek and walked into the living

room. "How exciting. Sounds like your day was more interesting than mine."

"Make yourself comfortable. I'll be right out," Nora called out from the bedroom. I plopped down on the couch and Luca threw himself next to me, a book already in his hand. He loved to read, and it was now our thing to read before we did anything else.

Nora worked nights at a bar, and I watched Luca and her little girl Lena a few times a week. It wasn't unusual for me to sleep on her couch because I was too tired to drag myself next door. We always joked that us meeting was fate.

"I might be a bit later tonight. We have a private function in one of the back rooms. Lena is already asleep. She didn't sleep much last night, so she was pooped," Nora said, dressed in her usual work outfit of skintight black jeans and a skintight corset. She refused to wear the short skirts that were part of the uniform, but she got away with it because she was a fantastic waitress and her boss loved her.

"You know I don't mind. It doesn't make a difference to me when you get home. I'll most likely be asleep anyway," I said.

She leaned over the back of the couch and kissed Luca's head, then mine. "I don't know what I'd do without you. Thank you for watching my babies."

"I love Luca and Lena more than anything. You know there's nowhere I'd rather be. Go to work already and leave us in peace. We have a few books to get through before bedtime."

"All right, all right, I'm leaving. Sounds like you have big plans. He's had dinner and a bath."

I waved at her, not looking up from the book that was open on my lap. "Not the first time I'm doing this. Go.

We'll be fine. And I'll call if anything happens. Which it won't."

"Good night, baby," she called as she walked out the door, not waiting for a response. Luca was already lost in the book.

I squeezed him to my side until he started to protest. I wasn't kidding when I said there was nowhere else I'd rather be. "One book, then you'll have to put your pj's on, okay?"

"Two books," he bargained, knowing full well I'd agree.

"Fine. But no complaining when it's time to get dressed."

He held out his hand and we high-fived on it. Eight books later he was putting on his pj's.

2

I rushed into the office, trying to wrangle my thick hair into a ponytail. The chair groaned when I dumped myself on it, and I exhaled in relief at sitting down.

I ended up staying at Nora's last night. She didn't get home until four, and I took the kids out for an early breakfast to let her sleep in until seven. She'd be able to get a nap in the afternoon when the kids were taking theirs; I didn't know how she survived on so little sleep.

"You have a stain on your shirt."

My body jolted at the voice, and I nearly ended up on the floor. Mason was sitting on the couch near the front door, looking like a king holding court. Why he wasn't in the garage doing his mechanic thing was a question to ponder later.

I followed his gaze that was currently locked on the front of my T-shirt. "Shit, I mean shoot, I mean how did that get there?"

"Looks like spew."

I pulled the fabric up to smell the stain on my chest. "Huh, I guess it is."

"Big night?"

"What? No! It's not mine."

"Right. I don't really care if you got drunk or not."

"It wasn't me. It's Lena's."

His stupid, Greek-marble-statue face didn't move a muscle, which, of course, meant I was getting more flustered.

"Not that she was drunk. She's only a toddler."

There was a slight tick in his cheek. "Since when do you have a kid?"

"It's my friend's. I babysit for her sometimes."

His face turned into a beautifully annoying marble statue again. "Right."

I fought very hard to contain the eye roll that threatened to break free. "Anyway, I should get to work. Wouldn't want to get in trouble with my boss."

"Did you place my orders?"

This time I lost my fight against the urge to roll my eyes. "Yes. Just like I told you I would."

Mason leaned forward and pointed at my screen. "What's wrong with the computer?"

I glanced at the spreadsheet on steroids he was currently looking at and sighed. "I don't know. Either Willa really likes neon green lines or the screen is broken."

"Have you tried turning it off and on?" he asked what must have been the most offensive and unhelpful question mankind had come up with.

"Yes, I have indeed tried that. But it didn't work," I said instead of throwing the screen at him, which was what I really wanted to do.

"Guess you better get that fixed, princess."

Oh, how I hated that nickname. I lifted my chin and channeled my inner ice-queen. It always paid to have her handy. "You know nothing about me. Just because you *think* I'm a spoiled little rich girl does not mean you get to judge me. Now, if you would kindly remove yourself from my office so I can get to work, I would appreciate it."

"Willa said you knew how to use a computer. If that's not the case, I can provide pen and paper."

He left before I could throw a pen at him. Or a paperweight.

The ringing phone provided a much-needed distraction. While I was talking to the customer, I pulled my shirt off and tried to get the stain out with a wet wipe I found in my bag.

While I had the receiver between my ear and shoulder, Landon opened my door. "I would say my timing has once again been spot on." He looked at the ceiling and grinned. "Thank you to the higher power who led me here at the exact right time."

I jumped at his voice and covered my front as best as I could with the shirt. I was wearing a red lace bra that I hoped he didn't get a good look at. "No problem, you're booked in for Friday at three. We'll see you then," I said into the phone.

I hung up and made sure my top covered the front of my body. "Doesn't anyone around here knock?"

He was standing in front of my desk, a big grin on his face, showing me his dimple. His hair was a mess today, the curls sticking up in all directions. It only made him more attractive.

"What do you want?" I asked.

"You gotta work on your customer service skills, chicklet. How about you offer me a donut?"

"I'm not wearing a top," I deadpanned.

He sat down on the chair in front of the desk and waggled his brows at me. "I know."

I tried to look stern but a smile slipped through. "I

guess it's my own fault for doing this in the office instead of the bathroom. Should have just let the phone ring."

"Hey now, I'm not complaining," he teased.

I chucked a pen at him, not liking where this was going. "What do you want?"

"Would you, pretty please, get us donuts from Sweet Dreams? Or their cupcakes. No wait, that's Willa's thing. I don't want her to think we replaced her. How about their vanilla slice? And brownies. They are amazing."

I sighed and rubbed my tired eyes. Guess I wasn't going to get much done this morning. "Fine. But only if you do something for me in return."

He sat up straighter and fluttered his eyelashes. "But, darling, I'm not that kind of man. And besides, I'm not allowed to touch you. Boss's orders."

"No, not that kind of favor. And tell Jameson I can look after myself, no need to threaten anyone to stay away from me. Can you work on another car for me tomorrow? I double-booked Mason by accident, and I really don't want to call the client—or tell Mason what I did."

"That's a pretty big favor. Not sure if one little sugar run is enough payment. And by the way, it wasn't Jameson that warned us off."

I ignored his last comment, too tired to think about why Mason would have warned everyone off. "I'll get you something from Sweet Dreams every day for two weeks if you help me out. But you can't tell Mason or the deal is off."

"Make it three weeks and you have a deal."

The lengths I would go to in order to avoid more of Mason's wrath were great. So, I did the only thing I could and shook Landon's outstretched hand while holding my top in a firm grip to my body. "Deal."

I pulled my hand back and narrowed my eyes at him.

"Why are you smiling at me like that? You look like you've had a stroke."

He shook his head, deranged smile still in place. "You know you might fool everyone else with your act, but I see right through you. Munchkin, I know you're smart. And you know how I know this? It's because I'm like the psychic Sylvia Browne. Only I'm male and still alive."

"Okay, Sylvia, why don't you go and do your psychic thing on the cars. You'll be busy for the next few days, so a little help from higher powers might come in handy."

He saluted me and went to the door. "Aye, aye, capt'n."

I couldn't stop the smile from spreading over my face. Maybe my day wasn't going to be so bad after all.

I HAD JUST COME BACK from my donut run and was full of sugar and happy thoughts.

Unfortunately, my hard-won equilibrium was ruined when Mason barged into my office without knocking and took over the room like only he could. There was something about him that took me completely off guard. And boy was he gorgeous when he was angry. His eyes went all stormy and his muscles tensed under his skintight shirt.

His coverall was pulled down to his waist, giving me a great view of his body. *And those arms*. I needed a moment to admire how good they looked when he was all tensed up like that.

"Are you even listening to me?" His hands were on his hips and the vein in his neck was pulsing. If he started breathing fire, I wouldn't be surprised.

And no, I definitely was not listening to a word he just yelled at me. I doubted it was anything important.

Honest to a fault, I shook my head. "Nope, I clearly wasn't. Did you have something to tell me that I actually need to know? Or did you just come in here to yell at someone?"

His face was about an inch from mine—*How did I not see him get this close?*—and he was breathing loudly. Even his breath smelled nice. Like peppermint. *Ugh, isn't there anything on him that I find disgusting? There was something wrong with me if I didn't mind him breathing at me. Gross.*

"Why are you staring at me?" he asked.

I stopped staring and leaned back in my chair. "I'm not staring. Just waiting for you to repeat yourself, so you can leave and I can do my work."

He closed his eyes for a few seconds and rubbed his temples. "This must be my penance for a misdeed in a former life. Because nothing I have done in this one warrants such a harsh punishment. I'm a nice guy. People like me. I'm the happy brother. Jameson is the brooder."

I raised a brow at him and tapped my hands on the desk. Happy my ass.

He looked at the ceiling and groaned. "Never mind. Just stay out of the workshop and stop giving Landon any ideas."

"What ideas, exactly, am I giving him? How to decorate his home? Or what he should have for lunch?"

He looked at me and narrowed his eyes. "You know what I mean."

"I clearly don't or I wouldn't ask." My voice was clipped.

"Just stay away from him."

"Says who?"

"Says me."

"Or what?"

"Or I'll have to give you a written warning."

I huffed. "What does that mean? A warning for what?"

"For distracting your coworkers."

"This is ridiculous. Don't you think you are taking this whole 'hate Stella and make her life hell' mission a little too far?"

"That's not what this is. I just don't want any distractions at work."

"And I'm a distraction?"

He didn't answer, but he didn't have to. God, he was such a jerky butt face. "Fine. I'll make sure not to distract anyone else again."

"Good. Then also make sure that you wear appropriate clothes." He looked me up and down. "Because this isn't working for me."

I could feel my face heat up. This was simply not happening. I had been told what to wear all my life and was not willing to put up with it anymore. The jeans and T-shirt I was wearing were appropriate wear for a garage. "Are you serious?"

"It's too tight. Now get back to work." He stalked toward the door, and I shot up from my chair.

"This conversation was more disappointing than an unsalted pretzel," I yelled my lame response at his back.

He didn't respond and walked through the door without turning around. And just in time because I was two seconds away from throwing myself at him. And not in a romantic I'm-going-to-ravage-you way, either. It was going to be more like a knee-to-his-balls situation.

THE NEXT DAY I was shutting down my computer when Maisie came barreling into the office. She was my other best friend and had gone to college with Willa and me. "Stella, you have to hide me. Now."

There wasn't much else to do but to usher her under my desk and put the chair back in place. Because that's what good friends did.

"I'll explain later," she promised from her hiding spot.

The huge desk was enclosed on three sides, which made it a pretty good place to hide. I was still standing in front of the desk, unsure what to do next, when a guy in a perfectly tailored suit strolled in. I didn't know where to look first. His artfully mussed dark hair, his gorgeous face, or his piercing blue eyes. I wondered if he was lost and if I should offer to show him the way back to the highway.

"Sorry, we're closed," I said. I was most likely giving off some major creeper vibes with the way I was staring at him. *But come on! When do you ever get the chance to look at a GQ model in real life?*

He was leaner than Mason and his hair was a little too styled. And maybe his arms weren't as nice, but it was hard to tell through the suit jacket. *And why the hell am I comparing him to butt face?*

"Where is Maisie?" he asked. Even his voice was perfect.

"I don't know. Have you tried the bakery three streets over?"

He raised a brow, most likely his version of an eye roll. "I saw her run in here."

Well damn, I didn't have anything to reply to that. Maybe I could pretend to be blind. But it was probably too late for that since he had to have noticed me blatantly ogling him.

I would never admit to anyone that I was even thinking it, but I was relieved when Mason stepped through the door with a scowl on his face. I even considered making him coffee. The feeling thankfully passed after a few short seconds.

"Can I help you?" he asked the new guy.

"Hi, I'm Oliver Thorpe," new guy answered and held out his hand. "I'm looking for Maisie."

"As in Thorpe Holdings?" Mason asked. There was something akin to awe in his voice.

"The very one."

Mason moved to stand in front of me and shook Oliver's hand.

"Nice to meet you. If you want to book your car, Stella is happy to do that for you," Mason said.

"No, she's not. Stella needs to close the office and go home," I answered. Mason really was nice to everyone but me.

"Thanks, but I don't need any work done on my car. Only bought it a few weeks ago," Oliver said. "I really need to talk to Maisie though."

Mason pointed at me. "Her name is Stella."

Oliver nodded. "Nice to meet you, Stella. Now can I talk to Maisie?"

Mason looked from me to Oliver. I pursed my lips, pretending to think. "Not sure when I've seen her last, sorry."

"Look, I saw her run in here. I know she's hiding so she won't have to talk to me," Oliver said.

Well, things just got interesting. I'd never heard of Oliver, and Maisie was an over-sharer. She told us everything. From what she had for lunch to how many times she had gone to the toilet that day. Her not telling me and Willa something set off all the alarm bells in my head.

He held out a handbag to me. "Can you make sure she gets this?"

I pushed past Mason, who refused to move to the side, and took the bag. "Sure. No problem."

"Thanks. And tell her I'll see her at my sister's birthday party."

He left without a backward glance. As soon as he started his car, I whirled around and dropped to my knees behind my desk. "Who the hell was that?"

Maisie was biting her lip and shuffled out from under the desk. She sat down in front of me and shrugged. "Just some guy."

"Liar. I want to know what the hell is going on."

"Nothing is going on. He thinks he has some sort of claim on me. But he doesn't. Now, can we forget this embarrassing scene ever happened? And promise not to tell anyone."

I grinned at her and pointed toward Mason. "Too late."

Maisie jumped up like Willa after she had a coffee and stared at Mason. "Shit. What the hell are you doing in here?"

Mason narrowed his eyes at her. "You're in my garage. If anyone should ask that question, it should be me."

Maisie wasn't easily intimidated and pulled herself up to her full height. She still had to look up to talk to Mason, but there was no more hesitation. "I'm visiting Stella to make sure you haven't made her quit yet."

"Still working on it," he replied, sounding too serious for my liking.

"Lucky I need the money," I grumbled, getting up as well.

"Have you finally been cut off?" Mason asked.

I clenched my teeth and balled my fists, my nails cutting into my palms. "Why don't you get back to whatever it was you were doing before you came in here?"

"Gladly," he drawled and left. As soon as the door

closed behind him with a loud bang, my shoulders slumped forward and I exhaled loudly.

"Seems like I'm not the only one keeping secrets," Maisie said.

"Ha, so you admit to keeping Mr. GQ a secret. I knew it."

Maisie shrugged and took my hand. "Come on, seems like we have a lot of catching up to do."

Crying to her about the butt wipe that was Mason Drake was just what I needed.

"Should we head to the Grill?" I asked.

"What kind of question is that?" she answered and grinned.

I laughed and squeezed her hand. "I missed you these last few weeks. No more overseas internships."

"I missed you too, Estrella, and there are no more trips in my future. Europe is overrated anyway. Now I hope you have your car here because Lincoln dropped me off."

Lincoln was one of her four roommates and a computer nerd who worshipped Maisie. Everyone but Maisie knew he was half in love with her.

"Lincoln, huh?" I teased her on our way out.

She groaned. "Don't start."

We got in my car and I sank into the leather seat, the familiar scent and feel calming my frayed nerves. Whenever Mason was close, my body decided to go from cold to hot, tense to boneless. It was infuriating.

"How did you manage to keep your car?" Maisie asked and sat down in the passenger seat.

"It was in my name, so my mother couldn't really take it from me. I'll have to sell it, though, if I don't get a job soon."

"Honey, you've got a job."

I waved her off and started the car. "You know what I mean. A job that won't end in a few weeks."

"Are you still staying at Willa's?"

I nodded and pulled out of the garage parking lot. "She's at Jameson's most of the time, so she's happy she doesn't have to pay full rent. But I have to find something soon. She lives in a one-bedroom apartment—and the couch is getting old."

The arrangement worked for now because Willa was on holidays for a few weeks, finally travelling like she had always dreamed of. The best part was that Jameson had gone with her. But once she was back, I had to find a place of my own.

We pulled up to the Grill and made our way inside. We used to go to the Donut Hole, but since Willa no longer worked there, the place wasn't what it used to be. Mainly we didn't get a 20 percent discount anymore.

Today definitely called for something like a burger and chips. Or pizza. But then again, every day should be a pizza day.

We chose a booth at the back, hoping to go unnoticed. Humptulips was a small town, and most people knew us, especially since my mother decided to run for mayor in the election that would be happening in a few weeks. She was the worst choice for the position, but it looked like she would win. Unfortunately, money made the world go round, and she had enough of it to never have to get off the carousel.

"Tell me what's going on with Oliver," I said, opening the menu I knew back to front.

"What the hell happened with Mason?" she asked at the same time.

Maisie had her "don't mess with me face" on so I didn't even try to pretend I didn't hear her question. "Fine.

I'll go first. Not that there's much to explain. It's simple really. Mason hates me. I hate Mason. We make each other's lives miserable whenever we run into each other. He thinks I'm a spoiled brat, and I think he has a chip on his shoulder the size of the Rocky Mountains. We only have to put up with each other while I work at the garage, so hopefully there won't be any casualties."

Maisie started laughing and I scowled at her. "Hey, stop that. I wasn't finished. I had a lot more to complain about."

Her laughter turned into a chuckle and she shook her head. "Oh, Estrella, there is no way he hates you. And besides, he's one of the nicest guys I've ever met. No way would he be mean to you. You sure you're not over-reacting?"

I put my hand up. "Don't even go there. This is not a case of pulling someone's pigtails because you like them. He is making my life miserable. And I'm beginning to think he has a point when he calls me princess. I did grow up in a mansion and never wanted for anything."

Except affection and love. But anything money could buy I had, which was starting to make me feel like the spoiled brat Mason thought I was.

Maisie put her hand up. "Stop. I know you. You are a good person and you work hard. You don't expect handouts. It doesn't matter where you come from. What matters is what you do with your life."

I still couldn't look at her, so I chose to study the ceiling instead. The paint was peeling, and it looked like there was a leak. "I know. It's just hard not to feel like a failure. Especially when the only thing I own are my clothes and a car."

"So, you're just like a lot of other college grads out there. Don't put yourself down like that."

"Thanks, Maisie." I finally looked at her. "You know I love you, right?"

"Of course you do. Why wouldn't you? I'm pretty awesome. Now let's order some food because I'm starving. I already waved Leslie off twice when she tried to take our order. If I do it a third time, she won't come back."

We didn't end up talking about Oliver but spent the whole time arguing about the ending of *How I Met Your Mother*.

3

"Has anyone seen a container of baby formula?" I asked the guys.

Landon's head popped up from behind the car he was working on. "What's it look like?"

"Like a container with the word formula written on it," I said.

Today was busy, and the last thing I wanted to do was search for the missing formula. I promised Nora I'd bring some with me when I went over tonight, so I bought it on my way to work that morning and left it in the staff kitchen.

Landon avoided looking at me and whispered something to Clay. Never a good sign, but I'd give him the benefit of the doubt. After all, what would he want with baby formula?

Landon came around the car holding something in his hand. "Is this what you're looking for?"

I recognized the silver tin immediately. "That's the formula. But why do you have it out here?"

"We ran out of creamer."

"O-kay... but that doesn't explain the formula."

"We thought it was just like milk. So, we used it in our coffee."

I burst out laughing. "How did it taste?"

He shrugged and handed the half-empty container to me. How much coffee had they been drinking?

"Tasted great. I didn't know it was yours. We thought you'd put it there to use. Sorry about that."

"You thought I put a container of baby formula out instead of creamer? Don't you think I would have picked up creamer or milk if I'd known we were out?" I asked, incredulous.

"Who knows how your mind works. You're still working here after three days, almost four. Nobody sane would last that long." Landon shrugged.

"Willa has worked here for a lot longer than that," I pointed out.

He grinned at me, his dimples popping out. "Just proves my point. She is the loopiest of them all. Has to be when dating Jameson."

I couldn't hide the smile on my face whenever I thought of my best friend and Jameson. "I think they're perfect together. And Jameson would do anything for her. They have a once-in-a-lifetime kind of love."

Landon made a gagging noise. "Stop, please, you're making me nauseous."

I slapped his arm. "Don't pretend you're not hoping to meet 'the one.'"

More gagging. "Haven't lost my mind yet, so the answer is no." He mock-shuddered.

"One day you'll remember this conversation when you find your 'one' and think, wow, Stella is such a wise person. And so pretty." I said the last part with a deep voice.

Landon laughed and put his arm around my shoulders, hugging me to his side. I grinned and sunk into him.

"Don't you have a clutch to fix?" Mason's gruff voice interrupted.

Landon let me go and turned around. "Sir, yes, sir. I'm on it." He disappeared back behind the car, leaving me alone with Mason, who looked as tense and put out by my presence as ever.

"Slacking off already?" he asked, his beautiful eyes sweeping my body. I thought I caught a flicker of interest before he resumed his mask of indifference. *But that's just crazy talk. He made it clear how not interested he was many times. He was probably just battling indigestion.*

"Wouldn't dream of it," I answered and batted my eyelashes.

He shook his head and left without another word.

I went back to my office and continued to screw up the spreadsheet Willa had started to keep track of all the orders. Her columns were so confusing; half the time I didn't know where I was. She told me not to worry about it since she could always fix it when she got back. But my pride wouldn't let me leave her with a long list of things to do, so I trudged on and tried my best to input all the information.

I lost track of time, and when my phone rang, I squinted at the display in confusion. "Hello?"

"Are you okay? How come you're still at work?" Nora asked.

"Why? What time is it?"

"Seven."

I jumped up and grabbed my purse. "I'm so sorry. I lost track of time. I'll be there in five."

She chuckled. It took a lot for her to get upset and not

even the prospect of being late to work would make her tell me off. "No problem. I'll see you soon."

I hung up, raced out the door, and crashed straight into a willowy blonde.

"Oh, I'm so sorry. We're closed." I pulled the door shut behind me and locked it. "Do you mind coming back tomorrow?"

She studied me and raised her brows. "You work here?"

"Yes? Why?"

She ignored my question and waved a hand toward the workshop. "I'm not here for my car. I'm meeting someone."

"Oh, okay." There was still a light on inside so someone must be in there. I thought everyone had left, but since the guys didn't always say goodbye, it was hard to keep track of who was still there. "Do you want me to tell them you're here?"

"That's okay. I'll go and find him myself."

"Nobody is allowed back in the workshop without one of the guys around."

She laughed and flicked her long silky hair back. "That doesn't apply to me."

I guess one of the guys used the workshop as his hookup spot. Didn't matter anyway. At least that was what I told myself when the image of Mason and her together popped in my head, causing a whole lot of not-so-nice feelings.

We were nothing to each other and I had to stop my confusing thoughts or risk following her into the workshop just to see who she was meeting. And I wasn't going to do that. No way. "Right. Well, then, good luck," I said.

Leaving her to it, I rushed to my car and sped back to

the apartment. Nora was already dressed and waiting for me.

"I'm so sorry, Nora. I hope I didn't make you too late."

She waved me off and kissed my cheek. "You're fine. Don't worry."

"I shouldn't be too late tonight. We only have two shows scheduled."

"And you know not to worry, since I will most likely crash here anyway."

She kissed Luca and Lena goodbye before she hugged me, forcing the air to escape my lungs. "I really don't know what I'd do without you."

I hugged her back just as tightly. "I love you and the little sticky monsters. You're my family."

We separated and she rushed out the door. After reading *The Very Hungry Caterpillar* for what felt like one hundred times, but was probably more like twenty, I put the kids to bed. I fell asleep on the couch and woke with a start when my phone rang.

"Yeah?"

"Is that how you answer your phone?"

I stilled when I heard her voice. She hadn't called me in two months. Two months that kept me in a land called blissful ignorance and wonderful denial.

"I was asleep."

"Of course you were. I thought I raised you to be a hard worker, but it appears you take after your father. It's a shame, really, after all the hard work I put into you."

Hot anger coursed down my spine at her insinuating my father had been lazy. How dare she insult his memory. My papá had been happy and hardworking when he was still alive.

He came from a poor Colombian farming family but fell head over heels in love with my mother when she visited the area he lived in. He followed her to the States but they weren't officially together. I never found out what happened between them, and since my mother refused to talk about him, I never would. But every memory I had of him was one of laughter and affection.

"What do you want?" I snapped and clutched a hand to my mouth, knowing what was going to come next. She would not let me get away with speaking to her like that.

"Watch your mouth. You might not live under my roof anymore, but I still own you."

Don't answer. Don't answer. Don't answer.

"I never want to see you again. I think I made that clear last time," I said.

Why in the world did you answer, you idiot?

Her cold laugh sounded down the line, mocking me. "Keep telling yourself that. We both know that's not true. You need me more than I need you. Don't forget, I know you better than anyone else. You'll come crawling back, like always. You're not made for hard work, and you'll be begging me for money soon enough."

There was no point in answering, so I hung up.

Instead of going back to sleep, I sat in the dark, brooding and wishing for things that could never be. Nora came back as I was pacing in front of the muted television.

She turned the lights on and yelped when she saw me. "What's going on? Did something happen?" she asked.

I released my clenched teeth and answered, "Sorry, didn't mean to scare you."

"Talk to me," she said and guided me back to the couch. We sat down and I turned toward her. "It's nothing. I'm just being dramatic."

She put an arm around my shoulder, pulling me into her side. "I hope you know there is nothing you can't tell me, and I will always have your back. Always. No matter what."

"I know. It's just family stuff. Don't worry about it."

I sighed, wishing I could unload on someone. But my problems were not for her to worry about. If there was one person who needed a break in life, it was Nora. That meant not adding to her worries.

"All right, Estrella, I'll let it go for now. But promise you'll come to me before you do anything stupid."

I snorted at the thought. "You've met me, right? The most illegal thing I've ever done is get a parking ticket."

She studied me for a few seconds and hugged me close. "How were the kids tonight?"

And there was yet another reason why she was one of my best friends and why I would do anything for her. She read me like nobody else; a topic change was exactly what I needed in that moment.

"They were great. Lena took a while to go to sleep, but Luca passed right out the second his head hit the pillow. How was work?"

"Same old shit. Too many drunks, not enough staff."

"You should really get a job somewhere else. Humptulips is small, but there are a lot of bars. Even if it's just to get away from creepy Clive."

"There isn't anywhere else that pays as well. There might be a lot of bars but only one strip club. And I can handle creepy Clive."

Unfortunately, she was right. It paid much better than anywhere else. If she didn't have a stalker, it would be a great place to work. But taking a pay cut would be worth it just to get away from him. Nora shrugged it off whenever I brought it up, not taking him seriously.

"This is one of the few times I wish I still had money," I

said and sat up again. "Then I could help you out and you could go back to school."

She shook her head. "Don't worry about me. I'm good. I have a roof over my head, beautiful kids, and food in the house. People are way worse off than I am. And the one thing I would never want you to do is go back home again."

I suppressed the hysterical laugh that wanted to escape. "You don't have to worry about that."

There was nothing left there for me, and the last thing I wanted was to see my mother again.

She got up and smiled. "Enough with the doom and gloom. Let's have a drink." Her head disappeared inside the fridge. "I think I still have a few beers somewhere in here."

Extricating herself from the appliance, she lifted two bottles up in triumph. "I knew it."

We toasted to the good things in life like wet wipes and James Fraser, and neither one of us mentioned families or work. In just a few months Nora had become one of my best friends and one of the reasons why I was reluctant to leave Humptulips behind.

4

It was Friday. Beautiful, long-awaited, glorious Friday. The week had been busy, and I was finally settling in. Mason was blissfully absent, and when he needed to place an order, he just emailed me a list. I decided to get comfortable and started playing 90s rock anthems, wore warm fuzzy socks when I was at my desk, and brought my teapot to work today.

The guys were booked out every day, so I started a waiting list. It didn't help that we were one man down with Jameson being away. Word had spread that Drake's Garage did the best rebuilds in the state, and after being in business for two years, all their hard work had started paying off.

It was almost closing time, and I was eyeing the clock on my desk. Willing it to turn to 5:00 p.m., I cringed when the door chime sounded, announcing a customer. I only had ten minutes to go.

"Welcome to Drake's Garage, how can I help you?" I said in my best customer-service voice, honed by many hours in front of the mirror. What could I say, I was a perfectionist. And getting the voice just right was a job in itself.

"I know my way around. No need to get up," the bombshell from the other day said, then walked toward the back door. I smiled at her, using my best customer service smile that hopefully masked my annoyance at the way she wrinkled her nose at me.

Her dress was so short, it barely covered her ass. Her hair was big, her lips bright red, and she used a heavy hand with her makeup. I felt bad for judging her; she could be a nice person after all. But I'd skipped lunch and was hungry, which always put me in a bitchy mood.

She breezed past me without another word. See if I cared that some people didn't know how to use basic manners. A hello would have done nicely. Much to my annoyance, I compared my ragged appearance with her perfect one. I eyed the stain on the front of my white blouse, a casualty from the donut I'd eaten this morning, and started scrubbing it with my finger.

Since it had been there for hours and was dry, my endeavor was pointless.

When the doorbell chimed again, I was ready to hide under my desk and tell whoever came inside that we were closed. It was 4:58.

"Welcome to Drake's Garage—" I started to say but words escaped me as soon as I saw who had come inside. My mouth was moving but no sound came out.

"I didn't believe Bayden when he told me you were working in the office of the garage where he got his car restored," my mother said, looking around the room with her nose turned up.

Her black suit was without a stain, fluff, or wrinkle, and her heels were shiny and unblemished, most likely brand new. Her hair was artfully arranged into a bun at the back of her head and her makeup was applied with precision, nothing smudged, nothing too bright.

One thing she didn't like was seeking out people, and her narrowed eyes made her displeasure clear. The fact that I hadn't been home in well over six months apparently hadn't sent a clear enough message. I was under the illusion that if I stayed away and pretended she didn't exist, I could stay under the radar. But it was only that, an illusion. And my ignorance had just caught up with me.

This wasn't the first time she had tracked me down. Last time I ended up hiding out at Maisie's place for a few weeks. The time before that I stayed at Willa's. They both knew bits and pieces about my mother, and I'm sure they put the rest together.

I pushed my chair back, careful not to make a noise and draw attention to myself. My mother was still studying the office, a room that was clean and modern, even though there were a few grease stains along the walls and floor. It was a garage after all, so stains were hard to avoid.

My body was coiled tight, my hands clutched together in front of my T-shirt. "Can I help you?" I croaked, my throat feeling like I swallowed sand. I hated that she still had so much power over me and could make me feel small with just a few well aimed words.

"You look ridiculous. What the hell are you doing? No daughter of mine is going to work in a dirty garage dressed in rags. As a receptionist no less. All the expensive schooling I paid for was for nothing. You truly are my biggest disappointment."

"I apologize but we're closed. If you need a service for your car, you can call or come back tomorrow."

She made a dismissive gesture and sneered at me. "As

if I would ever bring my car here. We're going home. I'm sick of your childish rebellion. It ends now."

My hands shook when I grabbed my bag. I was only too happy to go home. Just not with her. "You have no say over what I do anymore. Now if you'll excuse me."

With my head held high, I walked past her, keeping her in my sight the whole time. I almost made it to the door when I felt her fingers dig into my arm. "You think you can defy me? I decide what you do and where you go. You've had your fun; now it's time to come back home."

I tried to be strong and stand up to her but years of conditioning were hard to break.

"Let go of me," I pleaded, my voice no more than a whisper.

She ignored my pleas and dragged me outside and toward her car, a black Mercedes G Wagon. I stumbled after her, more out of habit than anything else. She wasn't strong enough to make me do anything anymore. But I was too stunned at her erratic behavior to pull away.

She liked to use well-placed verbal jabs and emotional manipulation. The fact that she had gone out of her way and come to the garage told me she was working on something that required my participation.

If I got into the car, there would be no more job at Drake's. Or girls' nights out with Maisie and Willa. Or babysitting Luca and Lena. I'd be right back to where I had been most of my life, locked up and forgotten in a cold mansion.

I dug my heels in and managed to stop our movement. My mother wasn't one to accept rebellion and pulled harder. I tried to free my arm and leaned back to use my minimal body weight to help me.

My arm slipped, but I stumbled and she used the momentum to push me toward the car. She opened the passenger door and shoved me in. I was too stunned at the physical assault that instead of jumping out of the car, I sat on the seat. After all, wasn't she the one who had always told me that a Connor never got physical?

"Why are you doing this? I'm not going to ruin your campaign. I promise," I pleaded. I was not above begging.

"Shut up," she sneered.

"I'll meet you for dinner. Tomorrow. But don't make me go with you now," I pleaded but she shut the door in my face and rounded the car.

"You're coming home with me. End of discussion," she said and slid into the driver's seat.

When she pulled out of the parking lot, I scrambled for the door lock. Everyone else in this town was driving a trusty old Ford truck, but my mother just had to get the latest G Wagon.

I was desperate, and the intricacies of new door locks were not going to stop me. With a bit of luck, I managed to unlock the door and open it. My seat belt wasn't fastened, so as soon as the door opened, I simply threw myself out of the car.

I didn't think my mother realized just how far I would go to get away from her. I could only imagine her surprise when she saw me disappear through the door.

I hit the ground and all air escaped my lungs. I rolled a few times, the concrete biting into my skin. My only saving grace was that we hadn't been going very fast; her tires screeched to a stop a few yards up the road. I rolled to my side to inspect the damage to my arm. Parts of my skin were torn off and it stung, bringing tears to my eyes.

"Stella?" someone called out.

I pushed myself up to sitting and turned toward the voice. Mason was running in my direction at full speed.

Tires spun out, kicking up gravel as my mother drove off, leaving me on the side of the road.

I was so relieved to see Mason, I started crying. He came to a sliding stop next to me and dropped to his knees. "Fuck, what happened? Do I need to call an ambulance?"

His hands hovered for a second before he put them around me and helped me up.

I gripped onto the front of his shirt, the contact grounding. "I'm fine. It's just a graze."

My voice sounded funny and I was wheezing, trying to force the air in and out of my lungs.

His eyes drifted over me. "Bullshit. You're not fine. I'm taking you to the emergency room."

I leaned against him with his arm around my waist, and he walked me to his car, putting me inside and buckling me in. He leaned closer, his eyes flitting over my face. "You still with me?"

I dropped my head back against the headrest and nodded.

He got in on the driver's side and started the car. The tires spun when he pulled out of the parking lot and raced down the road. I prayed we would make it to the hospital in one piece.

His head kept turning my way. "You're doing great. We're almost there. Just hang on a few more minutes."

Those were the longest few minutes of my entire life. My arm was on fire and tears were running down my face when we finally pulled up outside the emergency room. He jumped out and opened my door, putting his arm around me and helping me make my way to the door.

He sat me down in a chair in the waiting room, his touch light, his voice soft. "Wait here. I'll get someone to come out."

I was ready to curl up on the floor and start crying when he went up to the counter and left me by myself. My arm hurt, but I didn't think it was anything serious. I was a mess because of what had happened with my mother, her actions unexpected and out of character. After a few seconds, the nurse he was talking to put the phone to her ear and spoke into it.

He sat down next to me and traced a finger up my cheek, wiping my tears. "Hey, hey, it's okay. You'll be fine. They'll send someone out."

Of course they would send someone, because nobody ever said no to Mason. If he couldn't charm someone, he would intimidate them. In his world, he always got what he wanted. And for once I was glad, because the thought of sitting in a waiting room was making me shake even more. I wanted to go home and forget this day ever happened.

A nurse approached a few minutes later. After taking one look at my arm, she waved me straight through.

I was allocated a bed, then given something for the pain. Mason helped me lie down, his voice still soft, his manner so different from his usual coldness. Once he rearranged my pillows and pulled a sheet over my legs, I was sure they gave me the good drugs and I was hallucinating. He seemed to care what happened to me. And that was impossible.

Even though I knew that this wasn't real, and that he could go right back to hating me at any moment, I grabbed his hand and held on tight. He didn't pull back, but instead sat down on the side of the bed. We stayed like that until the doctor showed up.

He examined my arm, and after prodding and poking it, he came to the conclusion that nothing was broken, just bruised and possibly sprained. He wanted to do an X-ray to be sure, but I refused. It would cost way more than I could afford.

After a short and heated argument with Mason who wanted me to get the X-ray, a nurse put a dressing on and gave me instructions on how to care for the wound.

Once the doctor was satisfied I didn't have any other injuries, I was released with a prescription for pain meds. I guess the injury looked worse than it actually was, the shock of my mother trying to get me to come back home enough to send me into a panic.

In no time, I found myself back in Mason's passenger seat. We were parked in front of the pharmacy and he was looking at me. "I'll run in and get your medication. Do you need anything else before we go home?"

"I don't think so." I wasn't sure what I needed. But meds sounded great right now.

I took the paper bag he handed me when he came back and sat it on my lap.

We drove through Humptulips, but he didn't turn into any residential streets. I frowned when we left the town behind, wondering where we were going.

After a few minutes he turned onto a dirt road. A faded old wooden sign said "End Farm," the rest of the letters too faint to read.

The road turned out to be a long driveway that led up to a beautiful old farmhouse. The paint was peeling and a few of the windows were dusted over. It didn't hide the amazing architecture and beautiful details carved into the wood. It was surrounded by big trees and a new barn sat off to the side. I'd always loved living on a farm.

I only realized how much since I'd moved out. My mother's house, a palatial home that was designed to resemble a farmhouse, was twice as big as the one we were stopped in front of, but it always felt empty; after Gran and Pop passed away last year, there were a lot of empty bedrooms. And it was never a home, only a museum where I was never allowed to touch anything.

"Where are we?" I asked.

Mason turned the motor off and opened his door, looking back at me over his shoulder. "My house."

He came around to my side, opened the door, and unbuckled my seat belt.

"I can get it myself," I said, on edge and in pain.

He put his hands up and backed out of the car. "All right, I'll meet you inside."

He walked to the house and a giant black dog jumped down from the wraparound veranda to greet him, wagging his tail and licking his hands. "About time you showed up. Some kind of guard dog you are, Loki."

I could tell he liked his dog, and watched as he talked to him until they disappeared inside.

There wasn't anything else to do but follow him into the house. I walked past a row of dead potted plants that were sitting on the steps, and hoped I wouldn't join them in their fate. After all, we were out in the middle of nowhere, and nobody would come to my rescue if Mason decided I was too much trouble and went Norman Bates on me.

The house was half renovated inside. The hallway was freshly painted, and the wooden floorboards looked like they had been polished recently. A room to my right was still in pieces, the chandelier sat on the old floorboards, and the chimney was covered in ash and soot.

The next room didn't look much better, and I kept walking past the staircase and to the back of the house. My breath stuttered, then stopped when I saw the view.

Large French doors allowed for an uninterrupted view of a lake, surrounded by lavender fields. You couldn't see them from the front of the house because it was on a hill, and the fields were on the downward slope.

It was dark, but the moonlight was bright, illuminating the plants, giving them an ethereal glow.

I took in my surroundings and my steps faltered. I was standing in a huge living room that took up the whole back part of the house. To my left was a kitchen with light wooden cupboards and polished marble counters that looked brand new.

"I bought it for the view, but the house has a lot of potential," Mason said.

He was filling two cups with boiling water from the kettle, his dog sitting at his feet. "I made you tea. Don't get used to it though. I'm only doing this because you had a rough day."

"Wouldn't dream of it," I said and walked closer. "Your house is beautiful."

"Thanks. It's a work in progress. I have a guest bedroom upstairs that's nearly finished. You can stay there."

"Okay. But I still don't know why I'm staying with you."

He looked at the ceiling. "Can't you just accept when someone is trying to help you?"

"Depends on why you're helping me," I said with raised brows and walked into the kitchen.

He put the steaming mug on the counter in front of me. "I have to go and feed the animals. Make yourself at home. Or not. Just don't break anything."

Mason disappeared, and Loki wandered over and sat down by my feet, looking up at me. He was so big, I didn't have to bend down to stroke his head. "Hey, beautiful. I hope you're not as grumpy as your dad."

He groaned and laid down, curled up in a huge ball,

his nose tucked under his fluffy tail and his eyes closed. I sipped my tea, trying to come up with a plan. I had to find a way to get out of this house. Maybe Maisie could come and pick me up.

I pulled my phone out of my bag and hit my speed dial to call her. She picked up on the third ring, panting down the line like she had just run a marathon. Which was impossible because she hated exercise. "Estrella, what's up?" she whispered, barely getting the words out.

"Where are you and why are you breathing heavy and whispering?" I asked, forgetting all about the reason why I called her in the first place.

"I was hiding from Oliver and locked myself out of the house. I was on the roof so I had to climb down."

I chuckled. "How do you lock yourself out on the roof?"

"You climb out of the window and close it behind you. That's how you lock yourself out on the roof. The damn thing gets jammed all the time. Now was there a reason why you called, or can I get back to hiding out in my yard?"

I stifled the urge to laugh. "Hide away. I'll talk to you later."

"Later," she rushed out and hung up.

I didn't want to call Nora. It was one of her few nights off work. Willa was still away, and I didn't have any other friends. Guess I had to stay for at least one night.

My phone pinged with an incoming messaged, and I opened it to find a selfie from Willa. The bottom half of her face was cut off and all I could see of Jameson was his left ear and a bit of hair. The background was blurry, but I thought I could make out the Leaning Tower of Pisa.

The photo was so typically Willa that I missed her even more. Never could take a photo that was in focus.

5

It was still early, but I was exhausted and just wanted the day to end. When Mason came back in, he ordered pizza and we ate it on the couch while watching TV. I had no idea what we watched. My mind was full of toned arms, soft words, and gentle touches. Because I was living in an alternate universe where Mason was easygoing and supposedly cared about my well-being.

He almost made me forgot what a jackoff he typically was. This new version of him was hard to resist. He was attentive and nice. He joked around. He didn't insult me. Not once.

I wondered if he was the one who had an accident. Maybe he hit his head.

Loki was curled up on the couch in between Mason and me. His head was on my lap and I patted his soft fur with my hand. When Mason got up, Loki lifted his head but dropped it again with a groan when he didn't see anything exciting happening.

"You are the laziest dog I've ever met," I told him, smiling. I had never been allowed a pet. My mother found them too loud, messy, and smelly, and once she made her decision, there was no changing her mind. And I had more important things to fight for, like being allowed to go to school.

Mason came back with a bowl filled with half a gallon of ice cream. He smiled at me—I repeat, he smiled at me—and handed the bowl over.

I mumbled a thanks and dug in. Ice cream was on my mother's list of banned foods, so I hadn't had much of it growing up. She controlled my diet, my friends—which I wasn't allowed to have anyway, only beneficial connections—and my schedule.

She decided when I got up, which activities I was to partake in, and what I would eat. When I first moved out, I ate junk food for a month straight and didn't exercise other than walking to and from my car. It was one of the best months of my life.

If only she could see me now. She would probably have a heart attack and call me a disappointment again.

"I'll take it," Mason said, holding out his hand. I looked at it and frowned.

He wiggled his fingers. "The bowl. I'll take it."

I looked down and noticed I had eaten every last drop of the chocolate ice cream.

"That's okay. I can take it to the kitchen," I said, standing up. Or rather, attempting to stand up. Before I knew what was happening, I was without the bowl, and sitting back on my butt. Mason had managed to lift me up and sit me back down while simultaneously taking the bowl out of my hand. I had to admit I was a little bit impressed.

He walked off, leaving me in stunned silence. What the hell was happening here?

When he came back and handed me a bottle of water, I

stared at him but took it. "What are you doing?" I couldn't help but ask.

"What do you mean, what am I doing? Right now I'm watching a show. But since you're sitting right next to me, you would know that's what I'm doing because you're doing the same thing."

"I mean why are you being so nice to me?"

He turned to me. "Before Willa left, she made me promise to keep an eye on you. I didn't take her seriously. I mean what could there possibly be that I needed to protect you from? You are a pampered rich girl, who grew up in a mansion, and has people to do everything for her."

He put up his hand when I opened my mouth to tell him where to stick his opinions. "I was wrong. And I'm trying to make up for it."

Well, that shut me up fast.

He continued speaking once he noticed I wasn't going to say anything. "I saw you jump out of that car. Nobody jumps out of a car for fun. And you might not want to talk about what happened tonight, but I hope that eventually you'll trust me enough to let me help you."

I didn't have anything to respond. Nothing. He didn't seem to need an answer and turned back around to the TV. We spent the rest of the night in silence. It wasn't awkward. It was comfortable and I felt so relaxed that I nodded off, which was when he decreed that it was time to go to bed and walked me to his guest room. He even offered to help me up the stairs, something I declined. A girl had to keep some of her dignity.

"I'll get you something to sleep in," he said and left me in front of the guest bedroom. I watched him walk to the staircase at the end of the hall that led to the third floor before I turned to look at the room.

The first thing I noticed was the size. It was huge and the ceilings were high, making it look even grander.

A big bed was pushed up against the far wall, a blanket and pillow thrown on top. The floors were polished hardwood and the walls were freshly painted in soft beige. Two large windows faced the back of the property and overlooked the lavender fields. I couldn't wait to see them when it was light outside.

There was no other furniture in the room, making it look even bigger.

Mason came back, his heavy footsteps loud in the quiet house. He held out a pile of clothes. "I got you a T-shirt, sweats, and a sweater. There is no heating in the house yet, so you might need to layer up."

"That's more than enough. Thanks."

Mason stood in the doorway after handing over the clothes, brushing his hand over his hair and looking around the room. "I'm sorry it's not much, but I haven't had guests over yet."

When I didn't answer, he turned to leave, and my heart started pounding. *Just say something. Anything.*

"Mason," I called. *Thank the lord and baby Jesus, there were words coming out of my mouth.* "Thank you."

That's it? Thank you? After he peeled your butt off the asphalt, drove you to the hospital and now lets you stay at his house that's all you can say?

He waved me off. "It's fine. I have the space. I'll see you tomorrow."

Once I heard his footsteps fading, I went to the bathroom across the hall that he pointed out earlier. It was also renovated and boasted a beautiful clawfoot tub and a big shower.

The tiles were white and the cabinets a dark chestnut

brown, giving the space a simple elegance. He didn't add any colors or frills, and it worked. It was all him.

I changed into his clothes, the pants so big I had to roll them up a few times, and the T-shirt and sweater reached midthigh. I doubted I would be cold tonight.

After crawling into bed, I pulled the blanket all the way up to my chin. I drifted off with my nose in the sweater, smelling clean laundry scent and Mason.

6

"You stupid waste of space. Just turn off and we won't have a problem," I yelled at the tap that was gushing water.

It was the next morning and I was in the shower, trying to turn the faucet off. But it was stuck, and the now-cold water kept flowing over me while I tried to wrangle the tap. My teeth were chattering, and my plastic-covered arm was getting heavy. I had to hold it away from the spray and that was a workout for a five-minute shower, let alone for the fifteen I'd been in there for.

I gave up on the tap and opened the shower curtain to get my towel and reassess my situation. Or life in general. Because the way I was going, I wouldn't make it past breakfast.

"What the hell are you doing in here," I squealed when I saw a smirking Mason standing in the open doorway. I looked down at my naked and dripping wet body with wide eyes. And one of the first things that popped into my head was that I hadn't shaved in a while.

But who knew Peeping Tom over there would burst in without knocking? He ignored the color rising to my cheeks and walked past me to the shower, then reached inside and turned the water off.

I finally became unstuck and dove for the towel I had left on the sink and held it to the front of my body. At least now I was somewhat covered.

I tossed my wet hair across my shoulders, and it landed heavily on my back.

"What are you doing in here?" I yelled, too humiliated to acknowledge his help. Why was he still standing in the goddamn bathroom?

"Helping you," he said, raising a brow. "I could hear you yelling at the tap all the way to my room."

I nervously moistened my dry lips. "Get out," I said, my voice tight with barely controlled anger and humiliation.

One corner of his mouth was pulled into a slight smile. Neither one of us moved, and I noticed he was only wearing boxers. Really tight boxers. As in, you could see the outline of everything. A quite impressive outline.

And it was getting more impressive the longer I stared at it. I wanted to look away, but my eyes wouldn't comply. Instead, they greedily drank in all that was Mason. His muscled thighs. His defined abs. His perfect arms. Even his forearms turned me on. *Look away now, Stella. Look. Away.*

My eyes stopped before they got to his face, self-preservation finally kicking in. I backed my way out, holding the towel in front of me. As soon as I cleared the doorway, I sprinted to the guest bedroom and slammed the door behind me. Getting dressed was my top priority, thinking about what just happened a close second.

It was about two-point-five seconds after I closed the door that I noticed I didn't bring any clothes with me. I only had what I wore yesterday and what I borrowed last night.

A sigh escaped me at the thought of having to face Mason again, only dressed in a towel. If only Willa was back. Nora was busy with her kids; no way would I add to her crazy schedule and stay with her. And Maisie was in a house that was too full already. We used to be roommates, but my mother insisted I move back home after I finished college.

I was still playing the dutiful daughter back then and complied with her request. Maisie and I gave up the apartment we were renting and she moved in with some friends. They were nice but loved to throw a party. There wasn't a night they didn't have people over, which was a problem if you were sleeping on the couch.

I peeked out the door, and there was Mason, standing in front of me with a smirk, holding out a pile of clothes. I narrowed my eyes at him and snatched up the pile, disappearing back into the room. I wasn't feeling very grateful at the moment.

I got dressed in another set of Mason's clothes and made my way downstairs. When I got to the kitchen, he was standing at the counter, stirring something on the stove. He'd put on jeans—unfortunately—and a T-shirt.

Loki was sitting next to him, watching with rapt attention as he cooked breakfast. Mason looked up when I got closer. "Can you grab the milk out of the fridge?"

I nodded and went to the fridge to get him the milk and pray that he wouldn't mention what happened.

"We're having scrambled eggs and bacon," he said.

I put the milk on the counter next to him. "Anything I can help with?"

He gave me a sidelong glance. "You could get the plates and cutlery."

I looked around the kitchen and decided to start at the cabinet that was farthest away from Mason. I could still feel his eyes on me, and when I reached out to open the door, he said, "They're above the dishwasher."

I got the plates out and put them on the kitchen island.

"Cutlery is in there," he said and pointed to a drawer.

I got the forks and knives out and placed them next to the plates, at a loss at what to do next.

I watched him expertly wield a spatula and whip up breakfast. He even buttered my toast before he put it on a plate with the eggs and bacon.

I could get used to this. The thought scared me back to reality, and I asked, "Can you drive me back to Willa's apartment after breakfast?"

"Not happening," he said and went back to putting eggs on his own plate.

"What do you mean not happening? I don't want to stay here. You don't want me to stay here. The logical thing to do would be to drop me back home."

"No."

"No? That's it?"

He didn't answer; instead, he handed me my plate and sat down on the bar stool at the kitchen island.

"Why would you want me to stay? You don't even like me," I asked and took a seat next to him.

He looked up from drowning his bacon in maple syrup. "Is this about you showing me the goods earlier?"

I gasped. "You walked in on me. I didn't willingly show you anything."

He grinned and talked with a mouth full of food. "Then you should have taken a shower like a normal person, instead of screaming like the tap was going to jump off the wall and kill you."

"That's not what happened."

"That's exactly what happened. Now eat your food. You look like you could use a few more pounds."

"Did you just comment on my weight?"

He didn't look up this time, just continued eating.

I took a deep breath and tried to find my happy place. *I was not going to let him get me riled up. I was not going to stoop down to his level. I was not going to insult—*

Oh, to hell with it. I am totally going to insult him. "I don't have enough middle fingers to let you know how I feel about you," I said, having decided that taking the high road was for other, more well-adjusted people.

He continued eating, but I thought I saw his mouth quirk at my outburst.

"I'll have you know that I'm a perfectly normal weight," I said.

He glanced at me. "You've lost at least ten pounds since I first met you."

What a rude asshole to point that out. I had indeed lost a few pounds. Even though I still had some of my curves, something I had inherited from the Colombian side of my family, I did look a bit worse for wear if I was honest.

But I couldn't eat when I was stressed. And moving out of my family's house, despite my mother's objections, was taking its toll. And, hello, uncertain futures weren't exactly making me feel all warm and fuzzy.

I just couldn't believe that Mason had noticed. Or talked to me the way he just did. The anger lodged inside my chest and squeezed, making it hard to breathe.

I pushed my plate away and got up. "Why is it so important that I stay here? You hate me."

He pushed his plate back and turned to me. "Look, I don't hate you. And I apologized for being a dick. I was wrong and I'm trying to make up for it. Starting with taking care of you while Willa is away."

I guess he still felt obligated to make sure I was okay after promising Willa he would. Mason was loyal, and if Willa asked him to look after me, he would without thinking twice about it. I guess I was staying here at least another night. Not that it was a hardship since his house was beautiful and the bed I'd slept in felt like lying on clouds.

"Do you remember the first time I met you?" Mason asked, the sudden change of topic taking me off guard.

I thought back to the concert and nodded. "I think so. We met at the Music Factory."

"That wasn't the first time we met."

I frowned. I was sure I hadn't seen him before. "Yes, it was."

"We met the weekend before, when you dropped off a few things at Willa's apartment."

I thought back to that night and started feeling sick. I remembered that night. I was slowly getting my things out of the house but couldn't be too obvious about it. I was on another drop-off at Willa's.

"But we only said hello and that was it. How can you get shallow rich bitch from that?" I asked.

"You were talking to Willa outside before you left. You were telling her about some guy that hit on you over the weekend. You said that you would never stoop so low as to go out with someone who didn't even know the difference between Manili something and Choo Choo something else. And that he drove a rusty old car, which you didn't seem to like either."

Shit, I did say all that. And I remembered it clearly because I had been frazzled all day. Getting hit on by Barry was the last straw. The fact that he was driving a car that was older than my grandmother wasn't the real issue. I would have picked on anything because I thought he was a slimy scumbag.

"I couldn't care less if anyone knows the difference between Jimmy Choo and Manolo Blahnik. Honest. I was just tired and on edge that night. Barry was just the person to be at the center of my bitchfit." I looked at Mason, holding his eyes to make sure he knew how serious I was. "I'm not a superficial bimbo."

It stung that he had hated me all that time because of my thoughtless words. I had said a lot of things that I wished I could take back in my life. This was just another example of my mouth being a sprinter and my brain a marathon runner. The two never agreed on the same speed.

"How about a truce?" Mason offered. He looked sincere. And I really needed a break.

"Fine. But I still don't want to stay here."

"I know. How about a compromise? Stay for at least a few days. I promise to stop insulting you. I also won't ever mention seeing you naked again."

My face heated up and my eyes went wide. "You just mentioned it."

"Sorry. From now on I will never mention again that your beautiful naked body is burned onto my brain for all eternity. Do we have a deal?"

I gaped at his outstretched hand. He reached over and put my hand in his, then shook my limp appendage and grinned. "There you go, that wasn't so hard, was it? Now that we are basically friends, we should drink our coffees and watch mindless television together. Besides, you won't see me around much anyway. I have shit to do."

"Fine. I'll stay for a few days." I was too tired to continue to argue with him and the thought of having to walk back to town made me shudder.

7

"What are you doing up there? We're going to be late," Mason yelled up the stairs, causing me to drop my hairbrush.

I picked it back up, but instead of finishing brushing my hair, I placed it on the vanity. My hair was a lost cause at this stage anyway. I couldn't even wrangle it into a ponytail. I leaned out the door so he could hear me better and yelled, "You're the boss. I doubt anyone is going to tell you off for not starting at who-knows-what-time-it-is in the morning."

If only he knew how hard it was to get ready one-handed. My arm was still throbbing, and I tried not to use it too much. I poked myself in the eye with my mascara wand so many times my eyeballs were writhing in agony.

"You don't even open until eight," I muttered under my breath and grabbed a sweatshirt off the pile next to my bed. Mason had gone to Willa's apartment and packed some of my stuff.

All my clothes were still in a suitcase and I didn't have much in the bathroom, making it easy for him to pick it up. We managed to get along all weekend, and true to his word, Mason wasn't around much. Now it was Monday and we were apparently late for work.

"I like to be there early," he grumbled as he watched me stomp down the stairs.

"I'm ready."

"Why aren't you wearing your sweatshirt? It's cold outside."

"You try pulling on a sweatshirt one-handed. It takes time. Which obviously I don't have, since you insist on leaving before it's even light outside. So, let's go before I fall asleep again."

He took the sweatshirt from my hands and started threading my bandaged arm through first. He expertly pulled it over my head, then funneled my good arm through before pulling it down my body. Impressive.

"And here I thought you only knew how to pull clothes off," I said.

He tugged on a strand of my hair. "That is definitely my specialty, but it always pays to diversify. Any good businessman knows that."

I swatted his hand away and followed him outside. He opened the truck door and helped me up before walking around to his side.

We made our way down the pitch-black driveway, the only light coming from the truck's headlights. We passed the sign that still only said "end Farm," but I'd found out it used to say "Lavender Farm."

The drive to the garage took less than twenty minutes, not surprising since traffic in Humputulips was light in the middle of the night.

Mason helped me out of the huge truck, lightly holding on to my good arm. He left me standing in front of the office and disappeared inside the garage without a word.

I unlocked the office door and turned on the lights, all

the while thinking about sleep. After turning on the computer, I made myself a cup of coffee. Hopefully that would keep me awake.

I was tired and cranky for the rest of the day, the throbbing in my arm getting worse as the day wore on. I needed to type with both hands if I didn't want to be here late into the night.

As a result of my all-round grumpiness, I did the one thing I promised myself I would never do and was rude to a customer. But when he asked to change his appointment for the fourth time in the same day, I couldn't contain the snark from escaping. He complained to Mason.

I took another sip of my herbal tea and hoped it would calm my nerves. The package did say it was supposed to be relaxing. Because the last thing I needed was another confrontation with the man himself. I was tired and couldn't decide whether or not it hurt less to hold my arm up or rest it on the desk.

The heavy thump of boots announced Mason's presence right before he burst through the office door. Couldn't he do anything like a normal human being? The sturdy door could only take so much abuse before it splintered.

"I know we are supposed to get along and all that, but did you just yell at a customer?" he thundered as soon as he saw me.

I narrowed my eyes at him and took another sip of my tea. So far it hadn't done what the package promised and calmed me down. I should have added some of the whiskey I saw in the kitchen.

"He is one of our best customers," he continued when I didn't answer straight away.

I put down my cup and leaned forward in my chair.

"He changed his appointment four times. In the same day."

"And I repeat: he is one of our best customers." He stepped behind the desk and glowered down at me.

"Maybe you should take his phone calls from now on. He was almost as rude as you. Bet you two get along just fine," I answered, and regretted it immediately.

Mason's nostrils flared and I pictured him breathing fire. The thought made my mouth twitch, and I bit down on my tongue to stop myself from laughing. Because this was no laughing matter, and I had no idea what was wrong with me. Maybe the tea had gone to my head.

"I'm glad you find it amusing putting my business at risk."

I sat up straighter. "Hey, now, I have been working my butt off since I started. This was the first time I screwed up."

"You call him right now and apologize. And if he wants you to go over there and do it in person, you will."

My eyes widened and my mouth tightened.

He stared down at me, his eyes blazing. I pushed my chair back but didn't make it an inch before his hands shot out and he trapped my chair.

"Call him. And be ready to go home at six," Mason barked at me one last time before he left.

I swallowed the lump in my throat. I knew I had to pick up the phone and make the dreaded call.

No sense in delaying the inevitable. Calling the customer was the right thing to do.

The call went about as well as I expected. I had to listen to yelling, then cursing, and for the grand finale, I was told how incompetent I was. But he was going to still bring his car in, since he loved Mason's work.

The rest of the day went by in a blur. Mason came into the office just after six.

"You ready to get out of here?" he asked, studying my face, all his earlier anger gone.

"Just give me a minute to write this email," I said and nodded to my computer. "And then I'm ready."

He sat down on the couch, his gaze remaining on me. My body flushed at Mason's close proximity and attention, and I hurried to finish up.

"Thanks for making the call," Mason said when I grabbed my bag after shutting off the computer.

My steps faltered, and I locked eyes with him. "I'm sorry for being so unprofessional."

He grinned and put his arm around me, leading me outside. "Look at us giving this whole friendship thing a go, being all grown up and shit."

I scoffed but didn't push him away. Having his arms around me felt nice. I was in so much trouble.

8

The drive back to his farm was quiet, and I shifted in my seat the whole way. I was painfully aware of his every movement. His unique smell of oil, fuel, and hint of his cologne drifted over, and I fought the urge to lean in to get a better whiff.

Guess I no longer hated him. I'd finally admitted to myself that I felt attracted to him. Too bad he didn't return the feeling in the slightest.

When we parked in front of the farmhouse, he opened my door for me and helped me down. The touch felt comforting and I leaned into him. He shot me a questioning glance. I guessed I hadn't been as subtle as I thought.

Loki greeted us when we walked up the porch steps, and I patted him when he nudged me with his wet nose. Once inside, I went straight to the guest room and closed the door behind me.

I had to get my wayward emotions back under control before I could face Mason again.

At least staying with him meant my mother didn't know where I was. And wrestling with my feelings was a sacrifice I'd gladly make if it meant she'd leave me alone for a while. It didn't mean I wouldn't hear from her again. Her election campaign needed an intact family after all.

Not only had she married again last year for exactly that reason—and to someone only five years older than me—but she made the world believe that I still lived at home. Apparently, we were a wholesome, loving family. Which was so far from the truth, I felt like I was starring in my own scripted reality show.

I didn't sleep much that night, just tossed and turned and cursed my poor choices and shitty behavior. Maybe I really was the spoilt brat everyone thought me to be. The fact that I'd skipped dinner didn't help.

I was slow getting out of bed the next morning, and it took me longer than usual to put my clothes on. Tight jeans weren't the easiest to pull up your legs with one arm.

I took care applying some makeup, expecting Mason to knock on the door at any moment.

The interruption never came and there was even time to do my hair. I managed to put a few hairpins in and was pretty proud of my efforts. My arm was feeling better, but if I didn't have to use it, I wouldn't.

I left the safety of the bathroom, ready to face the world. What I wasn't ready for was a sleepy Mason who stumbled out of his room, wearing only his pants. I froze in the hallway, my eyes taking in all that was him. His hair was a mess, but it looked better than ever. My eyes swept over his defined stomach. He was pulling a T-shirt on as he walked, sadly blocking my view.

He grunted at me in passing about his alarm clock not working.

I went downstairs and fed Loki, then started the coffee. Mason joined me in the kitchen ten minutes later, looking a lot more awake and put together.

"You ready to go?" he asked while he poured his coffee into a travel mug.

"Yup," I said and held up my own travel mug.

The drive to the garage was once again quiet, but thankfully less charged than last night. He opened my door and helped me down. I didn't see him for the rest of the day.

I had a few invoices to catch up on, so I didn't notice how late it had gotten until I checked the time. It was nearly seven, and I was surprised Mason hadn't come to get me. He was usually ready to leave by six.

Shutting down the computer, I packed up my stuff and walked out into the garage to his workspace.

"That's it, baby, right there," a hoarse voice moaned.

I stopped dead in my tracks and my eyes went wide. Hell no, he didn't. He knew I was still in the office. He also knew I would eventually come looking for him.

I turned on my heels and left. I didn't need this. It also hurt more than I cared to admit to know he was hooking up with someone that wasn't me. No matter how far-fetched it was that he could be interested in me that way.

Once I made it outside, I took a deep breath, clenching and unclenching my fists. Once I had my anger and hurt under control, I called a taxi and waited on the sidewalk.

It was a weekday in Humptulips, so the taxi arrived in a few minutes. Luckily the driver wasn't anyone I knew, so I didn't have to make painful small talk.

I directed him toward one of the two motels in town and checked in. I needed a night off. I was ready to wallow in self-pity and eat copious amounts of snacks from the vending machine. By myself. Tomorrow I'd pull myself together and handle this like an adult.

He didn't know about my crush. And rationally I knew he was free to do whatever he wanted with whomever he wanted. Didn't mean his actions hurt any less. A break from being around him would hopefully put my head on straight again.

The small room I'd rented was covered in rose wallpaper, the bed clean, and the shower mold free. I had stayed there before and knew the owners wouldn't give out any information. They had covered for me many times in the past, and I was sure I could hide out there again.

I turned the TV on and dumped my purse on one of the two chairs in the room that sat next to a small table by the window. I splashed some water on my face and went outside to clean out the snack machine.

Not an hour later, I was sitting on the bed among empty wrappers, cursing my lack of self-control. After I got past the urge to vomit, I curled up under the blanket and passed out.

I woke up to pounding on the door and a plastic wrapper stuck to my cheek.

"Open the door," a familiar voice commanded.

I peeled the wrapper off and threw it on the bed. A glance at the clock showed it was just past midnight. I debated whether or not I should ignore the giant douchebag outside, but the pounding would wake everyone within a five-mile radius.

Trying to do the right thing, I dragged myself upright and pulled the blankets back. The chill of the room left goose bumps on my arms and I shivered.

"Stella, get up right now and open this door or I will do it for you," the angry jackass yelled. If nobody had woken up to the pounding, the yelling would surely have done it.

I pushed to my feet and padded to the door, yawning. The chain wasn't hooked up, so all I had to do was undo one lock and open the door. As soon as it was unlocked, it was pushed open all the way and I stepped back.

"I didn't say you could come in," I said and glared daggers at Mason.

"Get your stuff," he growled.

"No," I huffed.

Mason glowered at me. "Stella."

"Mason."

"Stella. Get. Your. Stuff."

"Mason," I mocked. "Get. Out."

Another growl, but he stopped saying my name like it tasted sour in his mouth and instead picked up my handbag, the only thing I had with me.

"Hey," I said and tried to take it off him. He ignored my attempts to reclaim my bag, then picked up my sweater from the floor and thrust it at me.

"Put this on. We're leaving."

"You are leaving. I'm staying."

He took a breath through his nose that sounded like a steam train, and he narrowed his eyes. "Haven't we already been through this? Willa asked me to look after you. So, until you're better, you're staying with me."

"Circumstances have changed. You are relieved from babysitting duty." I pointed at the door. "Now leave."

"Nothing has changed. You are still not able to do shit for yourself, which means you need to stay with me until you can."

"I'm fucking fine," I yelled and waved my arm around, unable to hide my cringe at the sudden movement.

"Of course you are."

Obviously done with our standoff, he swept his eyes around the room and after he was seemingly satisfied he'd picked up all my belongings, he stalked toward me.

I held up my hands and backed up. "Hold on. What are you doing?"

"I don't know what made you run, but I'll be damned if you get hurt because of your own damn pride. Now you have one choice. And that's to get in my truck."

Resigned, I pulled my boots on and stomped past him.

A few seconds later I was once again sitting in his truck, holding my handbag on my lap.

A muscle in his jaw ticked and his knuckles were white from fisting the steering wheel. None of those things deterred me from speaking my mind. "This is ridiculous."

"Finally, something we agree on."

"Nobody made you look for me. You are the only one who thinks I have to stay at your place."

"To keep you safe."

I wasn't willing to back down, more hurt by what had happened at the garage than I liked to admit. "Let's just get this over with."

9

"Why would you want to go back to my shitty apartment when you can stay at a castle?" Willa yelled, and I pulled the phone away from my ear or risked going deaf.

"You don't have to understand it. But I'm begging you, please call Mason and tell him to let go of his misplaced chivalry and let me go back to your place?" I asked, still holding the phone away.

"Fine. But I want it noted that I don't agree." Her voice was back to non-hearing-loss levels, and I put the device back to my ear. It was the day after what I dubbed "the incident," and I had finally called Willa. I had to get out of Mason's house, and getting her to call him was the best way to do it. He would be released from his promise and we could all go on our merry ways.

I sighed in relief. "Noted. And thanks."

"You sound off. I don't like it. Something happened. Did Mason do something?"

"Nothing happened."

"I don't believe you."

"Miss you, Wills," I said and wished she was here even

though she would pry the truth out of me in no time. I heard Jameson in the background and smiled when Willa giggled at something he said.

"Go and enjoy your holiday. And send me more photos."

"Will do. Love you, Estrella," Willa responded, already sounding distant as if she was pulling the phone away from her ear.

"Love you too."

We hung up, and I walked into Sweet Dreams to pick up the two dozen donuts for the meeting today. Turned out all the guys loved sugar, and there would be a revolt if there wasn't enough to snack on during their weekly meeting.

"Hey, honey. Be right there," Rayna called out from behind the counter. She was busy rearranging her display case, adding more sugary goodness. She owned one of the most popular bakeries in the area, and people often drove for over an hour just to buy her pastries.

"No rush, I'm on company time," I said and grinned. The more time I didn't have to spend in the office, the better. Things between Mason and I were tense. He was ruder than usual, and I was panic-inventing new words every time I talked to him. So far today, I had called him a two-headed cock puss—whatever the hell that was—a butt hanger, and a coddy-whompus asshole.

He acted like he never dragged me out of a hotel room, and I made sure he knew how displeased I was. The only feeling I now had whenever he was close was murderous rage. And maybe a little bit of attraction. But I was working on snuffing that bitch out.

I needed to eat away my feelings and Rayna was just the person to help me out.

"How is it going over there, anyway? I talked to Willa last week, but she didn't mention the garage."

"It's going. But what I really want to know is what you can recommend today?"

Rayna grinned at my topic change but let me get away with it. I had known her ever since Willa and I became friends. She was everything you could want in an aunt. She supported Willa without question, was nice to everyone no matter how crazy they drove her, and always had something on hand that was delicious to eat.

"I just made some lemon infinities. Want to taste one before you make up your mind? I need to know if they're any good anyway."

I held out my hand and nodded. "Yes, please."

She dropped a small pastry that looked like a mini figure eight into my hand. I took a bite and had to hold back the groan that wanted to escape. They were the perfect lemony, sugar goodness I needed in my life.

"They are amazing. You are a genius, Rayna. I'll take ten. And two dozen donuts. Just mix them up, you know how the guys are; they'll eat any flavor." My eyes roamed the shelves, greedily drinking in the different pastries. "And maybe a few brownies. Just in case."

Rayna grabbed a pair of tongs and started filling paper bags. "No problem."

"Put it all on the Drake account," I instructed. "And can you please make me a chocolate milkshake?"

She laughed and shook her head. "So, it's one of those days."

"Looks like I need to medicate myself with sugar and see where the high takes me."

Rayna put the bags on the counter and scooped ice cream into a metal cup. She put it under a mixer and added milk and her homemade chocolate syrup.

"All right, darling girl, here you go," she said and handed me my giant cup of diabetes.

"Thank you, Rayna, you are a lifesaver."

"I knew it was going to be a good day when I got up this morning. Another life saved, thanks to my incredible baking skills," she said and winked at me.

I laughed and grabbed the paper bags. "See you tomorrow."

I drove as slow as I could, dragging the ten-minute drive out to fifteen. When I got back, I parked in the employee parking lot, and after one last sip of my milkshake, I carried everything into the office.

"Finally. I'm starving," Landon said as soon as he saw me. He relieved me of all the bags and carried them to the meeting room, which doubled as Mason and Jameson's office and had a big enough table to fit everyone. I dumped my purse in a desk drawer, grabbed a notepad and pen, and walked into mayhem.

Clay was throwing something at Darren, who was busy taking a donut from the box on the table and ignoring everyone around him. Landon was moving the box around, while shoving one donut after the other into his mouth. Music was blaring from a speaker mounted to the wall, and Mason stood in the middle of the chaos, talking on the phone.

I sat down at the end of the table closest to the door. A quick escape was always a good idea, especially with Mason around. I watched the food disappear in less than five minutes and wondered where they put it all. The guys were all tall and muscular and looked like they worked out regularly, not stuffed themselves full of donuts.

"Shut up and listen," Mason said, and everyone settled at the table. "We have a few things to go through but not much time because we're behind on the Camaro."

A few groans followed his announcement, but after one look from Mason, it was quiet again.

"Clay, you get the Shelby. They finally brought it in, and it's in even worse shape than they told us originally. Engine rebuild and complete paint job for that one."

"Got it, boss," Clay said.

"Landon, how are you going with Teak's car?"

"I'll be done by tomorrow morning and can give Darren a hand with the Camaro."

Mason shuffled through some papers on the table. "Yeah, that sounds good. It's our priority right now. If anyone wants to do overtime, it's approved until further notice. And if you finish a project, you're on the Camaro."

I lifted my hand, and Mason's focus shifted from the guys to me. "Stella, you want to help with the Camaro?"

I once again fought the urge to roll my eyes and folded my hands in front of me, throwing a toothy grin at him. "We need to order more paint. There is no red or black left."

His irritation shifted to Clay. "That's your job to make sure we are fully stocked."

"Give me a break, man. We've been so busy I didn't even have time to scratch my ass, let alone remember to order paint."

"If you would stop using the garage as your personal fuck mobile, you wouldn't be behind."

"What are you talking about?" Clay asked.

"I found a pair of lace panties in my bay this morning. Spoiler alert: they weren't mine. Now look up what we're out of, and let Stella know."

"Sorry about that. We got carried away," Clay said with a grin, not looking sorry at all.

I felt all the anger escape me, like a deflated balloon. It hadn't been Mason hooking up, but Clay.

Clay got up. "You got it, boss man." He turned to me and smiled his boy-next-door smile at me. "I'll be by later."

"You can send her an email," Mason said, his face looking like thunderclouds were about to unleash their fury.

"I like to talk to people face-to-face. None of that online stuff for me," Clay replied and opened the door. "And you should maybe have a drink or three. You look tense, boss."

Before Mason had a chance to respond, Clay left the room.

"I'll put the list of upcoming jobs up on the board as usual. If anything urgent comes up, I'll let you know," Mason said and organized the papers spread out on the table in front of him.

I guessed that signaled the end of the meeting, because everyone got up without a word and disappeared. I was left in the room with Mason and jumped up to avoid any awkward situations. Before I could make a silent escape, I knocked my pen off the table in my haste to get out the door.

"I just talked to Willa," Mason said. "She said that you want to go back to your apartment and that you would be fine."

"That's what I've been telling you for days," I said, exasperated that it only got through his thick skull once he heard it from Willa herself.

"You can get your stuff tonight after work. The front door's unlocked, so just go in."

I shot up, banging my head on the table. "Fucking crap on a stick," I exclaimed and rubbed my head. "And why wouldn't you lock your door?"

"Nobody ever comes out there. And I have a dog."

"Because he is such a great guard dog. I don't think anyone has ever died from being licked too much."

"He's a smart dog. If someone just rocked up at the house and he didn't know them, he would attack."

"What if he knew the robber?"

"That's pretty much impossible. The only people that have been to my place and met my dog are Jameson and you. And I doubt either one of you is going to rob me."

I found my pen and shuffled back out from under the table. I didn't know how to respond to that. Mason was a social person. He had a lot of friends that he met up with often. Why hasn't anyone been out to his place? And why did that make me feel special?

"Right. Well, I guess I better get going. I'm sure Landon is done counting his paint buckets by now, and I should place the order as soon as possible."

I hightailed it out of the room and closed the door. Even though moving back into Willa's apartment was all I'd wanted, instead of euphoric, I felt crushed.

10

As soon as the clock hit five, I'd driven straight out to Mason's place to get my stuff. Luckily my car had still been parked in front of the garage and I didn't have to take a taxi.

Loki was beside himself when he saw me, and I think he peed on the porch in his excitement. I didn't clean it up. Mason deserved a smelly porch.

I grabbed my meager belongings and the apartment key Mason had left on the coffee table after getting my clothes from the apartment and drove back to Willa's apartment, where I was now hiding out.

I was snuggled into the soft blanket Willa kept on her couch, eating mac and cheese and watching the Discovery Channel, not football like I'd been forced to do for the last few nights. It was as close to heaven as I would get in my current situation of almost homelessness.

Nora was home tonight so I wasn't babysitting, but I made sure to spend some time with her and the kids. Bedtimes were always crazy, and I knew that's when she could really use an extra hand. So, I cuddled with the beautiful Lena while she put Luca to bed.

I also found out that Mason was the mysterious babysitter she'd found in my place. She sang Mason's praise until I was ready to move back in with him just so she would stop. Turned out he hadn't just watched the kids for her but also fixed her car and washing machine.

Which brought me to my current state of bliss. Because even though the mac and cheese were slightly burned, and Willa's apartment felt empty after having spent a few nights with Loki and Mason, it was nice to relax and not be on edge all the time.

I was sure I would go back to loving my own space after a few days. I'd been used to being lonely long before I met Mason, and I would be okay by myself now. I thought back to his surprisingly good cooking while I was picking the charcoal out of my dinner.

My phone vibrated on the table, but I ignored it. My mother had been calling me all day, leaving messages when I didn't answer. She would give up eventually. At least I hoped she would.

I was too keyed up to sleep but too tired to do anything but lie on the couch. It was just after ten when there was a knock on the door. I wasn't expecting anyone, and it was too late for a delivery. They probably had the wrong door, so I ignored it.

The knocking didn't stop but became louder and louder. I was afraid they were going to wake up the kids next door with all the noise and dragged myself off the couch to tell whoever it was to stop.

A look through the peephole showed me an unfamiliar face.

"Who is it?" I asked through the still closed door.

"Ms. Connor. Your mother sent me."

My heart sank. "It's late. Maybe you can come back tomorrow?"

Preferably when I wasn't home. I guessed my mother had found someone to do her dirty work. That didn't mean anything good for me.

"I'm afraid I can't do that. I need you to open the door."

Hell to the no. That would just make it too easy for him. "I don't know you. I'm sure you understand that I don't want to open the door to a stranger."

"If you call your mother, she will tell you that she sent me."

"I'm sure she will. But it's late and whatever she wants can wait until tomorrow."

There was a noise outside my door that sounded like he dropped something. I looked through the peephole again but couldn't see anything. Satisfied that he had left, I stepped back and turned around to go back to the living room. The door clicked open and I whirled back around. My mouth went dry and my eyes wide when I watched the stranger walk inside.

"What is happening?" I croaked out before I regained control of my body and sprinted toward the living room and my phone. This was not good. Not good at all.

I lunged over the back of the couch and my fingers grazed the phone before I was pulled back. My head hit the edge of the table, momentarily stunning me. My arm was on fire from hitting the couch, and I moaned in pain.

The guy grabbed me around the waist and helped me stand up but didn't let go once I was upright again. "Ms. Connor, I need you to pack your bag."

"Are you kidding me right now?" I wheezed, holding my arm.

He looked at me like we were having Sunday lunch and he hadn't just broken into an apartment. "No, I'm not kidding. If you don't want to take anything with you, we can leave right away."

I tried to roll out of his tight grip, but he didn't budge. He was a hulk of a man and didn't mind using his strength.

"I am not going to pack anything. Because *I'm not coming with you!*"

He sighed like I was the most annoying thing he'd encountered in a while. Which I probably was. I imagined people just did whatever the hell he told them to.

I felt myself being dragged to the front door and my impending doom. Back to being the good daughter that wasn't allowed to think for herself. Back to a colorless existence.

"Let's just get this over with," he said and pushed me out into the hallway.

"Hell no. Get your hands off me," I yelled, now hoping that I would wake someone up. I needed help and I needed it soon.

My salvation came in the form of Nora. "Get your hands off her," she yelled out of nowhere and swung a pillow at the guy.

He loosened his hold, and I dropped to the floor and crawled away. At least I tried to. The pillow attack wasn't very successful and he picked me back up, ignoring Nora who was still hitting him.

"Just kick him," I called out.

At least she listened and swung for his balls but only ended up grazing his shins.

"Let her go," she yelled and held onto his shirt. It was like a flea fighting a cockroach. Utterly pointless.

"Nora, caw da cups." My voice was muffled by the giant's hand that was now over my mouth. His other hand was around my waist in an iron grip, and he was shuffling us down the hall.

"What do you take me for? An amateur? I made a call before I came out here," Nora wheezed, not willing to let go.

"Wa da ya ma yoi afeady mai da ca?"

I wasn't sure if she could understand what I was saying since I was still talking into a hand.

"Why do you think it took me so long to get out here?" she asked. I guess listening to a toddler made her an expert in deciphering words.

"Beca ya didna hea mmm?"

"Nonsense. Of course I heard you. I have two kids. I'm a light sleeper."

We reached the stairs, and I renewed my efforts of getting away. Nora dug in her heels to help me, but we made no progress at all. It was pointless really. Maybe I should have saved my efforts for when he had to release me to get into the car. I figured that would be my best chance at escape.

Or I could make him hold all my weight. After all, I was no wilting wallflower, despite my recent weight loss. My ass hadn't lost any of its size, so there was still plenty to work with.

My thoughts of escape disappeared, and my eyes went wide when I saw Mason and Landon charging up the stairs.

"Than gah ya hea," I mumbled, my struggle momentarily forgotten.

"This better be a joke," Landon called out when he saw us.

"Took you long enough to get here," Nora complained. She let go of the hulk and stepped back with a smirk on her face.

"Let her the fuck go," Mason growled. He looked downright murderous. I had made him plenty mad over the last few days, but this was on another level.

Hulk man didn't read his clues too well, and even though he no longer covered my mouth with his hand, he was still gripping me to his side.

Mason charged forward, Landon right behind him. Hulk man finally loosened his hold enough so I could slip out and put some distance between us. I still wasn't sure what happened next, but all I could see were limbs flying every which way, and all three guys were on the floor. It didn't take Mason long to gain the upper hand, and he was soon smashing his fist in Hulk's face with a sickening crunch.

Guess the steroids must have fried Hulk man's brain because he didn't give up. He punched Mason in the side hard enough for him to let go. Hulk man rolled over, somehow kicking Landon on the way.

I backed up farther, reaching out for Nora. She took my hand and squeezed, shuffling as close as she could get, short of melting her body to mine.

Mason was back up before Hulk man got a chance to stand up, and this time Mason didn't look like he was going to go down as easily. His fists came down in quick succession, and I was sure something was broken by now. Landon got back on his feet, and instead of helping Mason, he tried to pull him away.

"Stop, Mason, he's out," Landon said, but Mason ignored him. He looked like he was in a rage, his eyes focused on Hulk man, his body strung tight.

Landon punched Mason in the side, and he finally released an unconscious not-so-hulky-anymore Hulk man.

"Don't do something you'll regret later. He's done," Landon said, standing in between Mason and Hulk.

Nora and I both gaped at the scene in front of us. I wondered if Hulk man was okay. I could still see his chest moving, but my feet weren't really working at the moment for me to go over there and check on him.

My almost kidnapper started groaning and Landon looked down. "At least he's still alive."

Mason turned and looked at me, his gaze assessing, taking in my disheveled hair and shaking hands. His mouth tightened. "You're back at my place."

Before I had a chance to reply, he closed the distance between us and I found myself crushed to his chest. My hands wound themselves around his body and I sank into him.

He buried his nose in my hair and held me close. I guess I could stay with him for one more night. The idea of being alone in the apartment after what just happened didn't really appeal. And staying with Nora and the kids would just put them in unnecessary danger.

And of course, hugging Mason wasn't a bad place to be. Maybe there would be more of that if I stayed with him again. Mason released me but stayed close, still breathing heavily.

Landon tapped his shoe to Hulk man's side. "Hey, wake up."

He only got a groan in return.

"Wakey wakey," Landon tried again.

Another groan.

"He didn't beat you that bad. You'll be fine in no time," Mason said, releasing me.

This time Landon got an angry groan in response.

"Hey, asshole. I'll help you stand up, and then you get your sorry fucked-up self out of here," Landon said.

He crouched down and grabbed hold of wannabe Hulk

man's hand. This time his eyes opened, at least the one that still opened, and he swatted Landon away.

"Fuck off, I don't need your help."

Landon stood back up and held his hands up. "Fine. Just trying to get rid of the trash in the hallway."

We watched Hulk man struggle to his feet. He was swaying back and forth. Once he was finally up and standing, he had to hold on to the railing.

He spat blood on the floor and started moving down the stairs. "Easy job, my ass," he said under his breath as he shuffled down the stairs, not looking back.

Landon flipped him off and turned to us. "You okay?" he asked.

Nora and I both nodded. We shuffled back into my apartment, and Landon and Mason followed closely behind. My bag was still pretty much packed, so all I had to do was zip it up and I was ready to go. No way was I staying at the apartment by myself, so I wasn't even going to argue about going back to Mason's place.

"He hurt you," Nora said with wet eyes and a shaky voice.

"I'm okay," I rasped out, not sure if I was. But I didn't want to worry her more than necessary.

Mason's eyes followed my every movement and I self-consciously brushed a hand over my hair.

"It's okay. Really. I hit my head when I was diving for my phone, but I don't think it was very hard." I tried to smile at Nora, but judging by the stricken look on her face, I failed to reassure her. "It's going to be fine. A good night's sleep and I'll be like new," I said.

"I don't believe you," she sniffled.

"You need to buy yourself a baseball bat," I said, walking back out into the hallway, locking the door behind me once everyone was outside. "Because a pillow? Really?"

She smiled at me sheepishly. "I heard you scream and panicked. It was the closest thing I could grab on short notice. It's not like you gave me any warning that someone might attack you tonight."

"My bad. I'll be sure to let you know a few days in advance next time."

"Thanks, I'd appreciate that," she said and hugged me gently.

I put my arms around her and hugged her tight. Because after all, hugs made the world go round. "I'll message you tomorrow."

She stepped back and wiped a stray tear from her cheek. "You better."

I followed Landon and Mason, who was carrying my bag, outside. Mason helped me into his truck, and we were on our way. I guess I was going back to Lavender Farm.

11

I groaned and rolled over, not ready to get up.

It was light outside, and I checked my phone for the time. I almost dropped it when I saw that it was past ten. After a lot of huffing and more groaning, I managed to shuffle out of bed and stand up.

Mason insisted I stay home today, and I wasn't in any state to argue with him last night. When we got back to his place, he inspected every inch of my body.

He even made me lift up my shirt. I had a small bruise on my side but was otherwise fine. My arm wasn't hurting anymore either, after I took a few painkillers. And other than hitting the table and being dragged around, I was fine. Things could have gone a lot worse for me if Mason and Landon hadn't shown up.

When he was done playing doctor, he sat down next to me and shook his head, his jaw a granite slab, his hands balled into fists.

"Shit, Stella, you scared the crap out of me. When Nora called—"

I put my hand on his leg. "Thanks to you and Landon, I'm fine. I owe you guys."

He inhaled deeply and before I knew what was happening, I found myself cradled on his lap.

"What are you doing?" I asked and tried to sit up.

"I just need to hold you for a while."

The sincerity in his voice made me still, and I studied his pinched expression. A warm feeling engulfed my chest, and despite my terrible night, I felt like smiling.

And what was a girl to do other than put her head on his shoulder and settle in when faced with an opportunity such as this?

"This is not something a normal parent would do. You do know this, right?" Mason asked after we had been sitting in silence for a few minutes.

I was momentarily confused about what he was talking about, having been lulled into a sense of contentment from being cuddled with such care. I started to believe this was real. "I know. But I can't change my family. My mother is who she is, and she does what she wants. Things are just going to get worse once she's the mayor."

"Has it always been like this for you?"

I took a deep inhale, and for the first time in my life, I wanted to talk about my unconventional upbringing. And at this stage, I had nothing to lose. Might as well go all in.

"When I was ten, I had this teacher at school. She thought I was a talented artist. She encouraged me to draw and even looked into scholarships for me. My mother found out about it. You have to understand that the only acceptable thing for me to study was either politics or law. Definitely not arts. Her response to the teacher's encouragement was to pull me out of school and get the teacher fired. I was homeschooled from then on. I was devastated but would never speak up or disagree. At least I managed to convince her to let me go to Winchester University."

I stopped, gathering my thoughts. I knew lots of kids

had worse upbringings. For all her faults, my mother never raised a hand at me. Her dragging me out of the office was the most physical she had ever gotten. She never even so much as touched me. Not to hug me or to slap me. That's why her actions at the office put me in such a state of shock.

"I'm not weak. But if you grow up where one person's word is law, you tend to go along with it. Especially when you are a child. I wasn't allowed to have friends, and the only time I was allowed to talk to anyone outside of our staff was when she had events for her campaign that required her family."

I snuggled closer, and Mason trailed his fingers up and down my back, offering me his silent support.

"Our housekeeper, Maria, was my only saving grace. She was affectionate, loved me like I was her own daughter, and never let me forget that there was more to life than pleasing my mother. She's the one who encouraged me to move out as soon as I turned eighteen. And once I met Maisie and Willa, my life changed for the better."

"I'm sorry, Stella. I didn't know," Mason said.

I lifted my head to look at him. "Not your fault my mom is a raging psycho."

"I feel like an asshole for judging you."

I put my hand on his cheek and he leaned into it. "Honest, it's fine. You apologized and more than made up for it tonight. I need to apologize too. I'm sorry for my knee-jerk reaction and just taking off. That was a shit thing to do."

"I still don't know why you just left the office without telling me."

My face heated up and I looked away from him. No way would I tell him the reason why I'd left. I needed to change the topic and fast. "Where did you learn how to fight like that?"

"I used to run car races with Jameson," he said, his stubble grazing my hand that was somehow still on his cheek, refusing to let go. "We often had trouble and I was usually the one sorting it out."

"You don't anymore?" I asked and looked up again.

"Jameson stopped as soon as he got together with Willa. Too risky. And I didn't want to continue without him. It was something we used to do a lot when we were younger but had grown bored of long before Willa came along. It was time."

He turned his head and kissed my hand, surprising me with the gesture. "Wanna watch some TV?"

"Best offer I've had all night."

He laid down on the couch, taking me with him. After he pulled me tight to his front, he turned on the TV and started a movie.

I didn't make it past the opening credits before I fell asleep.

He must have carried me up to bed, because I didn't remember walking up myself. The gesture was sweet, something I was beginning to think was Mason. The rude asshole was gone, in its place, someone that I liked a whole lot.

Since I was under strict instructions not to leave, I shuffled into the kitchen to start the coffee and make myself a piece of toast. Loki scratched at the front door and I let him in. His tail was going a mile a minute, his excitement about seeing me again making me feel warm and fuzzy.

"Hey, buddy, how about a piece of toast?" I asked and broke off a corner. "Just don't tell your dad."

Mason was strict when it came to his dog's diet.

Nothing fatty, no grains, and definitely nothing processed. But what he didn't know, he couldn't complain about.

After I finished my breakfast and coffee, I went outside with Loki. I hadn't had an opportunity to snoop around yet, and since Mason would be gone all day, this was my best chance.

I decided to start with the barn, since he seemed to spend an exorbitant amount of time in there. Loki ran ahead and disappeared through the half-open door.

The door slid to the side smoothly when I pushed on it. The barn looked almost new and smelled of fresh hay and animals.

I stepped inside and looked around. I could make out a donkey in one of the stables and decided to start my investigation there. He stuck his nose out when he saw me coming and searched my body for food. I giggled at his intrusion and looked around for something to give him.

There was a bag of carrots leaning against the next stall, and I went and got him a few. Judging by his reaction, I just made a friend for life.

The next stall was empty, the one after that held a goat with her baby. They were just as friendly as the donkey, and I bent down to pat them. The baby goat started chewing my sleeve and pulled me down farther, pushing my chest against the door.

When it became clear that a little goat was a lot stronger than me and wouldn't let go anytime soon, I slid out of my sweatshirt and left it with her. She seemed happy with her prize, carrying it around the stall, while doing little jumps and wiggling her tail.

After I caught my breath, I went to the next stall and was greeted with a litter of sleeping puppies. They had giant paws, and judging by the size of their mom, they were going to be huge once they were older.

I didn't want to wake them and stayed outside, even though I was dying to go in and pet them. They were adorable, and I was a sucker for puppies.

I eventually moved on and discovered a horse that seemed to be blind, a pony that had more hair than should fit on such a small body, and a few chickens who perched on stall doors and hay balls.

So this was Mason's big secret. Animals that looked healthy and well taken care of.

Loki followed me around the barn as if we did this walk together every day. I liked it. I was only ever allowed expensive horses. Some of them cost more than a lot of people spent on a house, so they didn't make for good pets.

And I didn't get to ride them. That was left to the staff. I always wished for a pony that I could ride through the forest, one of my favorite places on my family's farm.

And now I might not ever get to see the farm again. Especially not after the way things went down last night. I still didn't think my mother would just give up. But at least she no longer knew where I was. That was one thing I was sure of. Because if she did, she would have already been here to get me.

I finished my tour of the barn and peeked into the last stall. This time there wasn't an animal living there but a beautiful motorcycle. An MV Agusta, if I read the writing on the tank correctly. I didn't know much about bikes, but I knew I'd want to ride on that one. Maybe Mason would take me one day.

No wonder he spent so much time in the barn. There were a lot of animals to take care of. He was so different from the person I thought I knew. And every time I discovered something new about him, I liked him a little bit more. And at the rate I stumbled over new pieces of his life, it would be more than like and attraction soon.

I went back to the porch and laid down on the couch that was pushed up against the side of the house. It didn't take long for me to fall asleep.

Loki woke me, his wet nose nudging my cheek. "Mi amor, stop licking me."

The endearment had slipped out, surprising me. I didn't remember much of my papá who passed away when I was five, but he always called me *mi amor, mi vida,* and *preciosa*.

When he was gone, my mother banned everything from the house connected to him, and that included the language. I wasn't even allowed to learn Spanish but managed to pick up a few words in secret.

I didn't just lose my papá but part of my heritage, part of who I was. So, I held on to the few things that I still remembered. When Willa and Maisie found out how important it was to me, they started calling me Estrella, meaning star.

Shaking off a past I couldn't change, I stood up and followed Loki, who ran ahead a few paces and waited for me, only to repeat the process again and again.

I went back inside the barn, hoping the puppies were awake. To my utter delight, they were up and jumping around. I carefully opened the door and squeezed through the gap, keeping Loki outside and the puppies inside.

As soon as I stepped into the stable, the little hellions jumped on my legs and bit my shoes, overjoyed at having a new playmate. I sank down on my knees and gently ran my hands along their fluffy coats. They were soft and happy, making my heart sing with joy.

"Hello, my precious babies. And hello, gorgeous

mamá. Don't worry, I'll be gentle with them," I said to the dogs.

I didn't know how long I stayed, but when my knees got stiff and my top was soaked from the puppies sucking and chewing on it, I went back into the house. It was early afternoon, so I decided to waste the rest of the day with bad daytime TV and junk food.

The first part of my plan was easily set into motion, the second not so much, since Mason didn't seem to have even the smallest amount of unhealthy food in the house. I did notice he ate very healthy, which explained his out-of-this-world body.

I refused to give up my quest for unhealthy food and eventually found some expired marshmallows. Since they were 99 percent sugar and I was desperate enough to take my chances, I grabbed them out of the cupboard. I also took more painkillers and flopped onto the couch.

I was still sitting in the same spot, finishing off the last of the packet when Mason came back. It was after eleven and he looked tired.

"Long day at work, honey?" I greeted him and popped the last marshmallow in my mouth.

"Something like that," he said and collapsed on the couch next to me. The cushions gave way under his weight, and I was thrown to the side a bit.

"How was your day?" I asked and held up my cup of tea to stop it from spilling. The health freak didn't even have hot chocolate, so I had to raid his stash of herbal tea.

"Good. Long. How are you?"

I liked that he cared. Maybe a bit too much. "Feeling much better. Thanks for giving me the day off.

"What are you eating?" he asked and gave me the side-eye.

"Marshmallows."

"How did you get to the shops?" He was sitting up now, a scowl on his face, ready to yell at me. I could feel him gearing up for it. He was even taking a deep breath in when I interrupted him.

"Relax. Geesh, I was a good girl and stayed on the farm. I found them in the back of your cupboard."

"I didn't buy them. Did you check the expiration date?"

I waved him off. "They're all sugar. Basically impossible for them to go bad."

He sank back into the couch, mollified. "Just don't throw up in bed. The smell is a bitch to get out."

I snorted at the thought. My stomach was made of iron. I could pretty much eat anything. "Don't worry, your precious linens are safe."

He didn't respond and stared at the TV instead. I didn't even know what show was on, having zoned out a while ago and had instead scrolled through bodybuilder memes on my phone.

"I'll be out of your hair tomorrow. Things should be settled down by then."

Mason didn't seem to like that thought and got up. "I told you before, and I'll say it again: you can stay here for as long as necessary. I have plenty of room."

"And I said that I was fine and didn't need to stay here."

"Right, just like you were fine last night?"

"That was just a stupid coincidence. Won't happen again."

"For fuck's sake, how can you be so naïve?"

I got up as well, not liking sitting down while he was standing over me. Guess our truce was over.

"I'm not naïve. I just don't like being told what to do."

"I noticed. Too bad you make shitty choices and need someone to tell you when you do."

I balled my fists and got up on my toes, making myself taller. Not that it made much difference, since Mason was a giant and over six feet tall. Must run in the family since his brother was tall as well.

"Because you don't agree with my choices, doesn't make them shitty," I yelled. Damn it, and I was doing so well not shouting at him. Guess there was more calming tea in my future.

"Damn it, Stella, he could have taken you," he yelled back, running his hand through his hair, then yanking on it. "Your mother owns this town, and you know it."

I was surprised he knew how far my mother's reach extended. I guess it wasn't as much of a secret as I thought.

"Don't you think I know that better than anyone? And I also know there's no way I'll go back."

The last part was delivered rather dramatically, my voice high, my eyes wide, and my arms waving around wildly.

"Then let me protect you, instead of running the other way every time you see me."

He was getting right up in my face, his voice still raised, his body tense.

But I wasn't scared of him, never that. If there was one thing I knew, it was that he would never hurt me. At least not physically. His insults stung, his actions too, but he would never lay a hand on me. Of that I was sure.

"I'm not running the other way." I sighed, frustrated and tired. "But I won't let you talk down to me when I don't even know what your fucking problem with me is."

"My fucking problem? I tell you what my fucking problem is," he yelled. We were toe to toe, and I could feel his breath on my cheek and smell faint traces of his cologne.

I was standing in front of him, thinking if I should yell back or just walk away, when his lips were on mine and all the air left me.

My heart jolted and I melted into him. We were the perfect fit, his body curling around me, making me feel small and cherished. His kiss was soft, his touch gentle, his actions the opposite of his earlier fury.

He nipped and sucked and licked my lips until I opened eagerly. His tongue slipped inside and my whole body broke out in goose bumps. I felt like I couldn't get enough, pulling him closer by his shirt, even though every part of me that could possibly touch his body already did.

He pulled away and I moaned in protest. The sound died on my lips as soon as his mouth touched my neck, kissing a path down to my breasts. Every touch set me on fire, every kiss stoking the flame. He pulled my sweatshirt up and cupped my breasts. Not wearing a bra came in handy right now.

How could his kisses turn me into such a brainless mess? If that was a preview of what he was capable of, I was a willing participant. Even if it was just for one night. For tonight, I just wanted him.

He groaned and pulled away, his eyes still fixated on my breasts. His eyes wandered down to my stomach, and his face went from looking dazed to predatory.

I put my hand to his chest, my brain functions somewhat returning and telling me that this might not be the best idea. But since I was never one to miss an opportunity, my damn hand started to wander. I brushed across his chest and down to his abs, loving the feel of the hard ridges under my palm.

"Stella," Mason ground out.

My hand wandered even lower. "Mason," I answered as I grazed over his belt buckle, and then I was finally at my destination. He was big all over, and the bulge in his pants grew when I brushed against it. Encouraged by his response, I cupped my hands around him and stroked. I guessed the saying about big feet and big hands was right.

One moment I was the one in control, and the next I found myself on my back on the couch, Mason braced above me, his lower body pushed against mine. I writhed and hooked my leg around him, needing him closer.

"Whatever you do, don't stop," I said, ready to tear off my clothes right then and there.

I was dosed up on painkillers and marshmallows. This was going to happen.

He pushed my T-shirt up and carefully got my good arm out. He then pulled it over my head and threaded my injured arm through.

I wasn't wearing much and undressing me wouldn't take much time. Score for lazy dressers like me. His eyes hungrily roamed my body, looking ready to devour me. I shivered at the idea, not opposed to it in the least.

We could go back to arguing with each other afterward. He kissed the top of one breast, then the other. I was in a Mason fog, unable—and unwilling—to tear myself away from him.

The chemistry was unlike anything I had ever felt before. My body responded to every one of his touches, no matter how small. My pants came off next, and as soon as they were gone, I hooked my bare legs around him.

I was almost naked and he was still wearing all his clothes. I wanted to feel his skin on mine and mindlessly started tugging on his T-shirt, my attempts at undressing him less successful than his.

When it became evident that it would take a small

miracle to get his shirt off with one hand, he sat up and put his hand to the back and pulled it off in one swift move.

He came back down and his mouth found mine, his soft lips gentle, his tongue coaxing. I couldn't get enough of kissing him, of feeling his skin under my hand, and opened to him eagerly.

His hand slipped under my panties, and I was moaning as soon as he made contact, unable to stop the sound from escaping. Our kisses became wetter and deeper, and I arched into him, wishing I had two hands to explore instead of just one. I wanted to touch him everywhere, wanted to take his pants off and then pull him closer.

When his finger slipped inside, I nearly came undone. He knew just how to touch me to set me on fire.

Before I had a chance to process what was happening, his mouth was hot against the inside of my leg, blazing a trail up to my center. My underwear was gone soon after and his mouth found me. The sensation was almost too much, and when he added a finger, I came harder than ever before, sure that I was seeing stars.

That last part might also have something to do with me taking more than the prescribed amount of painkillers. When I came down, I was a boneless mess, unable to move or think. Mason was grinning up at me, looking very pleased with himself. He kissed his way up my body and leaned over me.

"Are you okay?" he asked, his finger trailing down my cheek. The gesture felt intimate and I didn't know how to deal with it after all the back and forth between us.

"I'm fine," I said, my voice scratchy.

He looked at me a moment longer and then got my underwear and pulled them back on. He found my pants and sweatshirt and did the same. I was too confused to do anything but lie there. The only movement my body would allow was to blink my eyes. I was fully dressed in less than a minute.

"Let's go to bed," he said and helped me up. He kissed my hand and held it all the way up to my room.

"Sweet dreams, beautiful," he said when we got to the door of the guest bedroom and gave me a light kiss on my lips. I blinked, waiting for him to deepen the kiss, but instead, he smiled at me and backed away. "I'll see you tomorrow."

He walked up to his room, leaving me in a post-Mason haze. And here I thought we were turning a corner.

12

THE NIGHT WAS LONG, I DIDN'T SLEEP MUCH DESPITE HOW exhausted I was, and I was more confused than ever. I went from hating Mason to wanting to crawl into bed with him. I needed my head checked because something seemed to be malfunctioning in there.

After only a few hours of sleep, I woke up way too early. But I wasn't getting out of bed while Mason was still here. I tried to fall back asleep, but my mind wouldn't shut off.

Why did he give me one of the best orgasms of my life and then just stop? Was I bad at getting orgasms? Did his equipment not work? Did he not want to have sex with me? And why are there no white and black M&Ms?

I would have had my mouth on him quicker than he could say blowjob. I wanted to wrap my lips around him and make him as much of a sated mess as I had been. What guy didn't want you to do that to him? The more I thought about it, the more confused I became. I was so stuck in my head that I didn't immediately hear the door opening.

The creak of the floorboards finally made me aware

that someone had just come inside. I played dead, ready to clock them if they tried to rob me. Or take me back to my mother. My eyes were still closed because I was too chickenshit to open them to see who it was.

Whoever it was didn't seem in a hurry because they stood next to the bed, not moving for what felt like hours, but was probably only a few seconds.

I heard rustling, and then I smelled a familiar aftershave. My body instantly relaxed, already trained to trust the butt-wipe who just scared the shit out of me.

I felt warm lips on my forehead and a strand of my hair being brushed out of my face. Before I could pull myself together enough to let him know I was awake, he was gone again, closing the door soundlessly behind him.

I sat up so fast I nearly pulled a muscle in my back. What. The. Hell. Did that just happen? Did he feel bad about last night? Was that the first time he had come in here? *Somebody give me some answers, or my head is going to explode.* I needed intel. Right now.

I fumbled for my phone on the nightstand and texted Willa. No idea what time it was where she was now, but questions had to be answered.

Me: *Wake up.*

Me: *Wake up. Wake up. Wake up.*

Me: *Don't tell me you put your phone on silent. You never put it on silent.*

Her response came a few minutes later.

Willa: *Different time zone, so lucky for you I wasn't sleeping.*

Willa: What's up?
Me: What do you know about Mason?
Willa: Oh no, what happened this time?

I THOUGHT this conversation was best had on the phone, and instead of texting back, I called her. She picked up before the first ring even finished.

"Estrella. Are you okay?"

"Hey, Wills, I'm fine, just need you to sort through the mess in my head."

She chuckled. "Hit me."

"Okay, so I should probably start with mom sending one of her goons to pick me up."

"She did what?" Willa interrupted with a high-pitched shriek.

"I'm fine. She didn't succeed. Mason and Landon showed up and kicked the guy's ass." I took a deep breath and continued. "Anyway, that's not why I am calling. So, I'm staying with Mason again because he insisted, and then we kind of fooled around last night."

Willa shrieked again. "You did what?"

"Oh my god, Willa, it was so good, I think I heard angels singing when I came."

"That's a good thing though, right?" Willa asked, sounding confused.

"Well, it would be, if he hadn't left straight after."

"Back up. So, he made you come but didn't get himself off?"

"Nope. Didn't even try. And believe me when I say I was ready for whatever he wanted. But he just put my clothes back on me and walked away."

"I'm confused."

"So am I. And then this morning he came in and kissed

me on the forehead. Kissed. Me. On. The. Forehead. So, get unconfused and help me figure this out. Because the more I think about it, the more I think I might just be really bad in bed. Not that we were in bed. Or even got to any part where I could reciprocate. He put me in such a state, I don't think I was doing much else but moaning and trying to get him to permanently fuse himself to my body."

"You like him."

"I'll admit I'm in lust. Serious, all-consuming, won't-let-me-think-of-anything-else lust."

Now she was laughing, making me narrow my eyes.

"This is not a laughing matter. Stop it," I said, my voice clipped. Did she not see how serious this was? "Don't you understand that the future of my vagina is on the line?"

She laughed even harder, and I heard the phone drop. I guess we were done with our conversation. Not that she had helped me much in my quest to sorting out my head.

I hung up and got out of bed. At my bedroom door, I listened for noise, but when the house stayed quiet, I ventured out of the room. I didn't know how to take what happened last night and this morning. And until I could dissect every single thing, I wasn't ready to face Mason.

It looked like he'd left right after he came into my room. The coffee machine was cold and the dishes sat on the counter next to the dishwasher.

He was a great cook but created a mess equal to none whenever he so much as made a cup of coffee. If we were actual roommates, I would have told him to clean up after himself on the first day. But since he was doing me a favor —no matter how much I didn't want to admit it—I bit my tongue.

I let Loki back inside and made a cup of coffee. Then I proceeded to mummify myself with a blanket and sat on the couch on the porch outside. Loki was sitting in front of me, waiting to see if I would let him come up as well. And of course I would, because why would I say no to my own personal heater?

I patted the space next to me, and before I had a chance to say okay, he was curled up on the cushion, head on my lap. I was going to steal Loki and take him with me when I left. And maybe I'd also take one of the puppies. Speaking of which, I should go and see if they were all right.

I sipped my coffee, loving the peace and quiet. The farm was in the perfect spot, not too far from Humptulips, but still removed enough to afford privacy.

The mountains loomed in the distance, the view breathtaking on a clear day like today. This was truly heaven on earth.

I wondered why Mason had bought the farm. He didn't strike me as a lavender farmer. And where did he get the money to buy it? It couldn't have been cheap. There was a lot of land surrounding it, and the house and barn were massive. Even though the house still needed some work, it was solid, and the necessary improvements mostly cosmetic.

When my mug was empty, I put it in the dishwasher and turned it on. My next stop was the barn, where I played with the puppies and tried to get my sweatshirt back from the baby goat. My attempts were unsuccessful, and I lost a shoe when I went inside the stall. I gave up when the little demon tried to eat my hair.

Loki followed me around, his tail wagging, his tongue lolling. I made sure to tell him how gorgeous he was and petted him in between escaping the demon baby goat and playing with the puppies.

It was midmorning when I went back inside the house and started looking for a vacuum. After opening a few closets and a door that led to the basement, I found an old dusty vacuum in the storage space underneath the stairs. It still worked, and I went through the whole house.

I had to empty the vacuum catchment out twice, and it was a pain to get the heavy old giant up the stairs one-handed, but I was determined and refused to sit around another day and do nothing. Especially not with Mason on my mind. Being idle wouldn't lead to anything good. My arm was healing well, and I was ready to stop being a patient and instead start pulling my weight again.

After I took a late lunch break with Loki, I searched for a mop and bucket. I eventually found them in the laundry room that was sitting just off the kitchen. It also had a new washing machine and dryer, and the floor was filled with at least a month's worth of dirty clothes. I rolled my eyes, wondering how many clothes the man-child had that he didn't have to do any laundry for so long.

So, I added laundry to my to-do list and put on a load before I started mopping the floors. The house was dusty from the renovations, and I had to change the water three times. But once I was done, it smelled fresh and I hadn't once thought about jumping Mason—or little Mason—as soon as he walked through the door.

Okay, that was a lie. Maybe I thought about it once when I was waiting for the bucket to fill with water. And when I mopped the living room. And then again when I wiped down the kitchen. Okay, fine, it was three times. But no more than that.

The washing was done, and I hung it up outside and put in another load. It was nearly dinnertime and getting dark, but Mason hadn't turned up yet. I wondered if I should start on dinner. I was pretty good at making mac and cheese. Or I could order pizza.

I ended up doing neither; instead, I turned on the TV and watched the news.

I looked up when the front door opened and Mason walked through. I was starving and cranky and nearly cried in relief when I spotted the takeout bags in his hand.

He was sorting through the mail when he walked in, but looked up when he heard me get up from the couch.

"Please tell me you're going to share that food," I said, my eyes on the bags. The smell told me it was Chinese and my mouth started watering.

"Grab some plates and a beer, and I might consider it," he answered, a teasing note in his voice. I wasted no time and dashed to the kitchen.

He had barely put the brown bags down when I was in the living room, holding out his beer.

"Thanks," he said and took it, giving me one of his smiles that made his whole face light up.

I stared at him, imagining what it would be like to run my tongue over the dimple in his chin.

Thankfully the smell of the food pulled me back to reality. I got the containers out of the bags, all seven of them, and took the lids off. After I shoveled a mountain of food on my plate, I looked up at Mason, who was watching me with a smirk.

"Don't judge me; you got most of my favorites," I said.

I moaned when I took the first bite, savoring the sweet and sour flavor.

The sound made his eyes heat up. His attention made me squirm and I chewed faster.

"Aren't you hungry?" I looked back at my food, hoping he wasn't expecting me to eat like a rabbit.

"I am. But I think I enjoy watching you more," he said and filled his own plate.

We ate in silence while watching a game, and I managed to finish the whole plate.

"Are you missing a sweatshirt?" he asked after we'd

both put our plates down and were watching the game. Well, he was watching, I was studying his profile, wondering if I should bring up what happened last night or just go to bed.

I didn't expect him to ask about my clothes. I'd already had a whole conversation about last night in my head, and I figured he would want to talk about it as much as I did. I was ready for the conversation but didn't know how to bring it up.

"A sweatshirt? What? Why? I mean no," I answered.

"I found one in the barn that looked a lot like one of yours."

"Wasn't mine. Nope. Definitely didn't lose it anywhere."

"I guess the shoe that was in there as well doesn't belong to you either? Size eight, pink?"

"I'm a size seven."

"Right. So, you also wouldn't know why there was an extra blanket in with the puppies and the goat was wearing Arwen's collar?"

"Who's Arwen?"

"The dog with the litter."

So that was her name. A bit strange for a dog, but okay. "How would I know? I guess you must have forgotten you did that last night. By the way, you must have also braided the pony's hair."

His lips twitched and he tilted his head. "Yeah, must have forgotten about that. My bad. That was a great idea I had there."

I tried to hold back the smile that wanted to form. "It was."

He nodded, his lips tilting up in a smile that lit up his whole face. "I'm known for my braiding skills."

I started laughing and flopped back onto the couch.

"Fine. I was out there, snooping. But all I found was a new barn and happy animals. No body parts or blood anywhere in sight. It was a bit of a letdown really."

He nudged my side. "Guess you haven't been to the basement then."

"So why do you have so many animals?" I couldn't help but ask.

He grunted noncommittally. "I wasn't planning on them to be honest. Love dogs and used to have a cat. But I work a lot, so it didn't seem fair to them. I found Loki on the side of the road when I was driving home one night. His leg was broken, and he looked like he'd been to hell and back. Was only a puppy. Got him to the vet who fixed him up. Nobody came looking for him, and it was either me or the shelter. So, I took him."

That was a decent thing to do. I was impressed, but no way would I say that out loud. "What about the rest of them?"

Mason settled deeper into the couch. "The donkey, Lola, belonged to the guy I bought the farm from. He was going to get rid of her. But she's old and nobody wanted to take her. So, she stayed. The pony, Wilbur, is from the circus. Knows heaps of tricks and is an escape artist. So always make sure you latch the gate properly. He hurt his leg when the circus visited last summer, and it looked pretty bad. The vet remembered me and asked me to keep him in the barn until the circus owners decided what to do with him. That was a year ago and he's still here. Arwen is one of my buddy's dogs. He didn't know she was pregnant until she gave birth. He lives in a one-bedroom apartment, so he asked me if I could take her. The horse, Fable, was dropped at my doorstep one night. No idea who left her there, but I kept her."

Oh no, it was official. Mason Drake was a good guy—I

was in so much trouble. I loved listening to him talk. I creepily watched his mouth the whole time he told me about his animals. I was also ready to reassess my life choices after listening to him.

I had no home, no animals, no job—not really, since the one I currently had came with an expiration date—and no money. Mason was only a few years older than me and had his life together, more than anyone else I knew. It was possible I grossly misjudged him.

"And now you've just taken in another stray," I said and pointed to myself.

"Not exactly a hardship."

I blushed and busied myself with putting away the empty containers. Dumping them all back in the bags, I carried them to the kitchen and heard Mason following.

Once I put away our leftovers, I threw the empty containers in the trash. The warmth at my back made me hold on to the edge of the counter. He was standing close enough that if I leaned back slightly, I would be flush against his front.

He trailed a finger up my arm, his touch light, his intentions clear. Did I really want to go there again?

I answered my own question when I turned around and tilted my head back. "Don't start this if you don't intend to follow through."

He leaned down, his lips a breath from mine. "The real question is, are you willing to see where this is going?"

I lifted my hand and slowly curled my fingers on the nape of his neck to hold him in place. I needed this kiss as much as my next breath. Instead of wasting more words, I got up on my tippy toes and closed the distance between us.

I felt the velvet warmth of his kiss down to my toes, my body instantly ready and aching at the contact. I was not usually this easily turned on, but Mason managed to get a response from me by just breathing in my vicinity.

He took charge, and I kissed him back with urgency, taking the kiss deeper, opening up to him, and struggling to hold back my moans every time his tongue touched mine.

His hands moved under my sweatshirt and skimmed my sides until they stopped just below my breasts. We broke the kiss and he stepped back. "Let's take this to the bedroom. I want to do it right this time."

I nodded, incapable of denying him. Didn't matter where he was taking me, I would have agreed as long as he was there with me.

He held my hand again as he led me up the two flights of stairs to his room on the third floor. I hadn't been up there before and was curious what it was like.

When I walked in, my eyes went wide, and I tripped on a pair of shoes. The bedroom took up the whole top floor, his room not as big as the width of the house, but still about the size of three normal-sized bedrooms.

The entire back wall was made up of windows, giving him an uninterrupted view of the lavender fields and mountains beyond. There were two doors coming off the left side, one leading to a bathroom, the other to what looked like his closet.

A king-sized bed was pushed up against the wall opposite the windows, making it the perfect spot to enjoy the view. He didn't have much furniture other than a nightstand and bed, but I could see the potential. There was enough space to add a sitting area and a desk. And if he added a few pictures, it would look a lot more like a home.

"I haven't had a chance to buy much furniture," he said, watching my reaction.

I squeezed his hand. "Mason, it's beautiful."

He looked at his feet. "Thanks. I always wanted to have a room like this."

I stepped in front of him, never letting go of his hand. "The whole house is amazing. You did an incredible job with it. And this room is everything."

He lifted his gaze and I saw a flicker of doubt in his eyes. "You think so?"

"I know so. I can't believe you did all this yourself."

"Jameson helped as well."

"I'm sure he did. But it's still your house and your hard work that put it together. It's okay to be proud of it."

He tugged on my hand and leaned down to kiss my neck. I shivered at the contact and he led me to his bed. "I'll show you the rest later."

I moaned my agreement, and he kissed me and walked me to the bed. He pulled my sweatshirt up again. "This needs to go."

I sat down on the bed and shuffled back, leaning up on my elbows. Mason followed and didn't waste any time; he buried his face in my boobs, worshipping each one with kisses and licks. I writhed underneath him, feeling like I was going to explode if he didn't stop teasing me.

"Mason," I moaned. "I need you."

His eyes were glazed over with lust, his breathing labored. "I'm not finished yet."

I pulled his pants down over his ass, making sure to brush my hands against him. He pulled them the rest of the way off. His boxers followed right after. I was still wearing pants, my impatience growing to explosive proportions.

"Please, stop teasing me," I whimpered, his hands roaming over my skin, making me tremble.

"Patience," he whispered against my stomach, while

pulling my pants and underwear down at the same time. His mouth and tongue forged a blazing hot trail down my body.

He entered me with one finger, then two, and then his mouth joined in. I was ready to come undone right then, but when I was about to topple over, he stopped.

"No," I wheezed, my body one big wanting mess.

"I want to be inside you when you come," he said and opened his nightstand, pulling out a condom. "Last night was just for you. But tonight, I want it all."

His words made my chest expand and my insides warm and I watched with hungry eyes as he rolled the condom on.

His body was back over mine and he kissed me again, this time hungry, wet, and deep. He slowly guided himself inside me, stopping when he felt me tense up. I knew that he was big, but actually feeling him inside was pure ecstasy. He gave me time to adjust and slowly kept pushing in, until he was fully seated inside.

He started moving with gentle strokes, bringing me back to the brink in a few short moves. My body trembled and my lips quivered. I mumbled out incoherent words, and then I fell over the edge.

He followed me right after, exploding inside me with a guttural roar. I was a boneless mess. The only thing that seemed to work was my arms that held him to me in a tight embrace. I couldn't even feel my injury anymore; the only thing on my mind was Mason.

He was heavy, making it hard to breathe, but I wasn't ready to let him go yet. He brushed kisses across my face, and I sighed with happiness. Every time his lips met mine, my heart turned over in response. I inhaled deeply, trying to get rid of the gooey feelings his touches evoked.

"Let me up, baby, so I can get rid of the condom," he whispered against my ear before he nipped it.

I grudgingly let him go, knowing that whatever this was would be over as soon as he left the bed. We could have fun together, but I would save us both the embarrassment of waking up next to each other.

Mason was not a relationship guy, and I had no illusions where this was going. Or not going, in our case. My modus operandi was retreat, and I had perfected the skill over many years. It was an instinctual reaction; my body was ready to sprint from the bed before Mason had even left it.

He kissed my nose one more time and went to the bathroom. I spotted my underwear on the floor and got up and put it on. When I saw Mason's discarded shirt, I pulled it over my head. It was so big on me, it went almost to my knees.

It smelled like him, and my emotions were raw enough that I needed something of his to keep with me tonight. I padded out of the room when I heard the toilet flush, already wondering if a repeat of what had just happened was in my future. We could be friends with benefits. I'd pitch my proposal to him tomorrow.

13

Turned out Mason didn't agree with my plans. The first indication that he wasn't feeling all warm and fuzzy about last night was his sour mood. He refused to look at me when I came into the kitchen the next morning and just glared at the coffee pot.

I, on the other hand, was looking at him as much as I could without running into things. Now that I knew he could back up his delectable body with some serious moves, I couldn't tear my eyes away.

He hadn't shaved, and the scruff on his face and his sleep-mussed hair nearly made me throw my pride out the window and jump him. *Oh, who was I kidding? I would definitely forget about my pride if he had given me any indication at all that he was interested this morning.*

But I didn't even get one of his mumbled good mornings that sounded more like gah.

All of my attempts to talk to him were ignored. In fact, he made an obvious effort to ignore me. Now this whole roommate thing was going to get even more awkward.

Before my mood plummeted further, and since I wanted to remain floating on my pink cloud of sexual bliss, I decided Stella version 2.0 would tackle the awkwardness and just get it all out there—and I would do it in the car where he couldn't get away.

I doctored my coffee to be 80 percent milk and 20 percent coffee, and we silently left the house. It was chilly outside, and I cradled my coffee mug, hoping to get some warmth from it.

When we pulled out onto the road, I decided it was going to be now or never. "I had a great time last night," I started, watching him for his reaction. Or rather his lack of one. He didn't even acknowledge that he heard me. "And if you'd be open to it, I was thinking we could be friends with benefits."

I nervously sipped my coffee while he stayed quiet. I watched him and waited for a response that never came. When we pulled into the garage parking lot, I had downed my whole cup and needed to use the restroom.

"So, what do you say?" I asked when he parked his truck.

"No."

I hated his one-word answers. Especially when they were no.

"Why not? Isn't an arrangement like this every guy's dream?"

"If he just wants to get laid, then yes, it is." He finally turned his head to look at me, and I gulped at the intensity of his eyes. "And how do you think this should work? We fuck when the mood strikes? But we can see other people?"

My stomach dropped at the thought of Mason with someone else. If I was honest with myself, I also wanted more than just friends with benefits with him. But that wasn't an idea I let myself entertain for too long. My life was too complicated right now and I didn't even know how much longer I'd be in Humptulips.

"We'd have to agree to not see other people while we're doing this," I said.

"You mean while we're doing each other."

"Yes, exactly." I felt hopeful that maybe he would agree on an arrangement. Didn't he see that this would be the perfect solution? We could both get something out of it. And I wasn't ready to end whatever we had between us. The thought of never being that close to him made a stabbing pain shoot through me.

He inhaled deeply and opened his door. I leaned forward and caught his sleeve to stop him from getting out before I had my answer.

"Mason?"

"No," he said again and left me sitting in the cab of his truck by myself. I realized that he really was angry with me, because he didn't even open my car door. And he always opened my door for me, even when we were slinging insults at each other.

I pulled up my big girl panties—or in my case, my sensible white cotton panties with purple hearts on them—and went inside. The office was quiet because it was the ass crack of dawn and nobody would be here for a few hours.

I used the time to catch up on what I'd missed. I had a bunch of messages and phone calls, but it didn't look like anything major had happened while I wasn't there. The evil part of me wished that they had really needed me, so Mason would see that I did contribute something useful to his business. The thought was petty, but I felt so worthless and rejected that I would take any form of recognition at this point.

It didn't take me long to straighten out orders and catch up on emails and messages that the guys had left on my desk. I kept finding sticky notes whenever I moved something. Every note made me smile, since it was never just a simple message. The last one I found was "If you read this, we might not be alive anymore. Donut supplies are low."

The excuse was good enough for me, and I decided to go see Rayna. Decision made, I grabbed my purse and left the office. It was still thirty minutes until we opened, and I could get there and back in that time without a problem.

Rayna was as cheerful as ever, and she greeted me with outstretched arms and a kiss on my cheek. "There she is. I was just talking about you. How's your arm?"

I scrunched up my face and glared at the arm in question. "It's good. Hardly hurts anymore."

She went back behind the counter, and I walked up to the display case to find out if she had anything new today.

"Who were you talking to?"

"Huh?" Rayna asked, already distracted with icing some red velvet cupcakes.

"You said you were just talking about me."

"I was talking to Willa. She said that you were having problems. You should have told me. I'd be happy to help. I have a two-bedroom house."

I never even thought to ask Rayna, but she was right. Her place would be a great idea. If only leaving Mason's would make me feel better. He wasn't only a great guy, the chemistry between us was combustible. And I wasn't ready to just walk away yet.

"Thanks so much for the offer Rayna, but I'm okay at Mason's for the moment."

She studied me before nodding. "Okay, Estrella, but let me know if that ever changes."

The offer was purely her; she was willing to help at a

moment's notice. I always wondered why she wasn't with anyone. I'd never seen or heard about her being with someone. She was like a big sister to Willa and always took care of everyone. She deserved to be happy.

"So, what are you having today?" she asked, breaking me out of my head, where I was making plans to set her up.

"Can you make up a few bags? Just put anything you want in there, as long as you include donuts as well."

Rayna was quick to select a few things, and I went back to Drake's after promising her that I would call if I ever needed something.

I might have to take her up on her offer, after all.

When I got back, all the guys were in the office. I opened the door and stepped inside. "Hey, what's up?" I asked, and every head turned my way.

"Are you okay?" Landon asked and hugged me. But instead of his usual crushing embrace, he lightly placed his arms around me and patted my back.

Next was Clay, then Darren, both equally as careful. "Let me know if you need anything," Darren offered.

I put my hands up when Landon stepped forward for what looked like another hug. "I'm fine. Really."

I was met with a roomful of skeptical eyes and wiggled the bags that I still had up in the air. "I got donuts."

That was sure to distract them. And what did you know, it worked. As soon as they spotted the logo, they started going through the bags.

"Why did you get so much?" Clay complained. "That means at least an extra hour at the gym today."

I shook my head at them. At least now I knew how they stayed so fit despite their terrible eating habits. "You know you don't have to eat them all now. I can put the leftovers in the fridge for tomorrow."

Landon looked at me, horrified. "Hush, you sinner. That's just blasphemous. This needs to be eaten while it's fresh."

I debated whether or not that was worth an answer, when he started suggestively licking his donut. All the guys groaned and left the office.

I sat down at my desk and unpacked my supplies for the day, trying to ignore the noises Landon was making. Once he was satisfied he wasn't going to get another reaction out of me, he went back to his bay.

I decided to message Nora to see if she needed anything. Tonight was one of the nights she usually worked, and I could go over there now if she was willing to pick me up.

Me: *Hey chick, you still need me tonight?*

Nora: *You should be resting. Don't tell me you're back at work.*

Me: *Of course I'm at work. Where else would I be? *ten smiley faces**

Nora: *So, I guess I need to fess up eventually.*

Me: *Yes?*

Nora: *Mason is on babysitting duty tonight. He asked me if I needed someone. Please don't be mad.*

Mason was still babysitting?

Nora: *You're mad, aren't you? Why are you not texting back?*

Nora: *Estrella?*

Me: *I'm not mad, just disappointed.*

Nora: *Now I know that you're definitely mad.*

Me: I'm still coming over. This is my gig.

Nora: You can both come over. The kids will love it. I can't just cancel on Mason. I'd feel terrible that he already changed his plans only to cancel on him last minute. And he seems to like being with the kids.

Me: Fine. But I'm in charge.

Nora: K. I'll see you soon.

DAMN IT ALL, I forgot to ask her to pick me up early. Guess I had to wait for Mason to put down his tools and come and get me since apparently we were going to the same place.

The office was too quiet and there were no sounds coming from the garage. The noise level was usually enough to have to turn the volume on my phone up to the highest setting so I could hear it ring. But once the guys were gone for the day, it went quiet. The sudden silence felt deafening.

My phone pinged with an incoming text and I opened it, hoping it was Willa. It wasn't. The message was from my mother who was saved in my phone book under *don't pick up*.

DON'T PICK UP: *I think you have been slumming it long enough. Time to come home.*

MY THUMB HOVERED over the keypad. If I replied, she would think she finally got to me. If I ignored her, she might send someone worse than the last guy to come and get me. I mulled over my options and finally started typing out a message.

. . .

Me: I'm not coming home. You can stop sending your lackeys.
Don't pick up: I expect to see you at dinner tomorrow.

A JOLT WENT through me at the thought of dinner. It was a big night for her campaign, and since she was still going with the wholesome, loving family picture for her voters, I was expected to be there. It had been planned since she first started her campaign. But since we hadn't been in touch in a while, I forgot it was happening.

Me: I don't think I'll be able to make it.
Don't pick up: You'll show up or your little friend and her kids will be without a place to live.

HOW THE HELL did she know I was friends with Nora? I never talked to her about anything other than the campaign. At least when I was still talking to her. I swallowed to dislodge the lump in my throat. This was bad. She never made outright threats.

I had to make sure Nora was okay. She had gone through enough and didn't need to worry about a place to sleep at night. I guess I was going to her pretentious dinner tomorrow.

Me: I'll be there.
Don't pick up: I'll send a dress and car.

. . .

Of course she would. Because she liked to have complete control. Which was why me moving out and not talking to her anymore made her an irate mess.

Good thing I didn't have to deal with her. I'd leave that to her husband. He was as dumb as a piece of string—no offense to the string—and would probably have no idea what was going on in the first place.

I was chewing my lower lip and pacing the office when Mason came inside.

"You ready to go?" he asked, wiping his hands on a rag.

"I'm coming to Nora's with you," I said, daring him to argue with me.

"If you're up for it," he said and dropped the rag on my desk despite my glower. "But I'm also happy to go on my own."

"I'm fine."

He studied me for a few seconds and nodded. "Let's do it."

I was still reeling from my conversation with my mother when we pulled up in front of Nora's apartment complex.

"If you clench your teeth any harder, you might crack one," Mason said and got out of the car. To my surprise, he opened my car door and helped me out.

I didn't want to let go of the hand he offered me once I was standing next to the car. His big hands were calloused from working on cars and motorcycles, which were in direct contrast to my manicured ones.

We were polar opposites on almost everything, but the way I felt when I was near him wasn't something I had ever experienced before. He made me madder than anyone had ever managed, but at the same time, he made me feel alive and free. And most important of all, cherished. At least when he wasn't mad at me.

He dropped my hand and walked inside ahead of me. There was no way to get out of dinner tomorrow, and I just had to stop worrying what might happen and accept that I had to go.

With that resolve, I followed Mason inside. He stopped in front of Nora's apartment and knocked.

Luca was barreling down the hall as soon as Nora opened the door.

"Macon, Macon, you came back. I knews it. Didn't I say he will comes back, Mom?"

Nora smiled at him and nodded. "You did say that. And I bet he is just as excited as you for another playdate."

Mason's whole demeanor changed when he looked at Luca, and I couldn't help myself but stare. Mason started smiling wide and crouched in front of Luca.

"How are you, little dude? Did you get the present I gave your mom for you?"

Luca high-fived the hand Mason held up and nodded, his hair flopping back and forth at his exuberant movement.

"I dids, and Mom said you can help me puts it together."

I looked at a smirking Nora and tilted my head in question when her eyes met mine.

"It's a Lego plane," she said, and the corners of my mouth tilted up.

Willa and I got Luca a Lego dinosaur for his last birthday, not thinking that the thing came in pieces. Something which was obvious to everyone else who ever bought Legos, since part of the fun is putting it together. It took Luca, Willa, and me three weeks and a lot of sweat to assemble it. A few random pieces were left over but Nora hid them before Luca found out.

I guess that was another point for Mason, since he noticed what Luca liked and had bought him something that made him happy. I just hoped Mason was good at putting Legos together.

"Luca, why don't you get your pj's on, and then you can play with Mason and Stella?" Nora said.

Luca was excited enough about the prospect of not one but two people to play with that he raced off to his room to get changed.

I held my arms out, and Nora handed a babbling Lena over. She snuggled into my neck and started blowing raspberries. It made me giggle and kiss her chubby cheek.

I looked up and my eyes met Mason's; he was staring at me with soft eyes. It was one of my favorite looks on him. As if he wasn't attractive enough on a normal day, the softness made him irresistible.

"The kids have had dinner already, but they can have some yogurt and strawberries for dessert. I should be home around midnight tonight," Nora said and put her jacket on. "Call me if there are any problems. I'll make sure to check my phone regularly."

"Nora," I said and raised my brows. "How many times have I watched your kids?"

She pursed her lips and rolled her eyes at me. "Not enough. Never enough. But I promise only to text you a few times tonight. I'm trying to get better."

And wasn't that the truth. Before I came along, Nora had a nanny that charged her half her night's earnings and invited her boyfriend over most of the time. Something that Nora only found out after we became friends, and I noticed her nanny's visitor.

She fired the nanny, and I offered to help out until she

found someone new. As far as I knew, she hadn't found anyone yet. Not that I wanted her to. I loved her kids and it felt good to be needed.

"Estebella, are you going to puts the airplane together?"

I was sitting on the couch, bouncing Lena on my lap, when Luca ran up to me with a few Legos.

"Mason really wants to be the one to build it with you, but Lena and I will watch you guys from the couch," I said.

"Good. Lena can'ts come down 'cause she likes to break my toys," Luca said and went back to his room to get the rest of the box. He dumped the contents on the rug in the living room, spreading them out.

Mason sat down next to the pile and pulled the instructions out of the box. He read the first page for a while; his forehead creased.

Ha, guess it isn't as straightforward as he thought. This was going to be entertaining.

"Okay, bud, how about you look for this part here," he said and pointed to a large Lego piece that looked like it would form the body of the plane.

Lena was getting grumbly, and I walked up and down the living room with her. She was almost ready for bed, but Nora always tried to get her to stay up until seven so she wouldn't wake up too early. So far, she hadn't had much success, and Lena's wake-up time of five in the morning hadn't budged.

I watched Mason gently coax Luca into putting the right pieces together, without making him feel like he wasn't the one doing all the building. I couldn't tear my eyes away from him. He was sitting next to Luca, sorting through the pile in front of them, smiling and looking carefree.

I gave Lena her bottle and she settled into my arms. She was such a good toddler, and I was always reluctant to put her down once she was asleep. I loved holding her, especially when she cuddled. I'd never thought about having kids. Besides the obvious lack of a partner, I also never thought it was something I wanted. Now I cherished every moment I spent with them.

"Lena is ready for bed," I said when she finished her bottle and got up from the couch. "Do you want to say goodnight to her before I put her down?"

Luca got up and I bent down so he could give her a sloppy kiss and a cuddle, and Mason gave her a kiss on the forehead.

I carefully placed Lena in her cot and closed her door. When I got back, Mason was helping Luca clean up. I stayed out of the way and listened to their easy banter.

"If I was a dragon, I fly Mommy to the Malsidives. She said if she could goes anywhere that's where she wants to bees," Luca said and looked at Mason expectantly.

"If I was a dragon, I would watch all the football games in the country. Because I wouldn't have to pay entry and could fly from one place to another. Like a road trip, but in the air," Mason said.

They noticed me standing at the edge of the hallway and living room and Luca jumped up and waved at me. "Esteballa, what would you do if you were a dragon?" Luca asked.

I walked over to him and kneeled down to his level. "I would make Rayna bake me everything she could think of and eat it all. Since I would have a big dragon stomach." What I would really do is fly far enough away so my mom couldn't find me. The Maldives sounded like a great idea.

Luca laughed at me and told me I was silly. We ended

up chasing each other around the living room. Mason watched us, his eyes still soft. I melted a little more.

I caught Luca and tickled him. "Okay, little man, time to brush your teeth. It's almost bedtime."

"Can I stays up for ten more hours, please?" Luca asked when I guided him to the bathroom and got his toothbrush.

"Sorry, buddy, no can do. Your mom said you have to be in bed by seven thirty."

"Awww, but Esteballa, I likes to stay up really wate."

"I know you do, buddy. But not today, okay?"

He sighed a long and drawn-out sigh and took the toothbrush I held out to him.

"Not fair," he grumbled and started brushing his teeth. It was more a case of brushing his lips and tongue, but it would do. After he asked a few more times—read: fifty-three more times—if he could stay up another ten hours, he was finally in bed.

Mason was on one side of the bed, and I was squeezed in on the other, Luca in the middle, grinning from ear to ear. He told us we both had to read him a story and stay in bed while doing so.

I just couldn't say no to his crooked grin. The kid was going to be a heartbreaker when he was older. His dark hair was falling around his face in curls and his blue eyes sparked with mischief. Nora was going to have to deal with a lot of teenage drama once he started dating. I just hoped I was still around when that happened.

"Goodnight, buddy," Mason said and did a fist bump with Luca after we finished reading a story. We had to keep our voices down since the kids shared a room. But Lena usually didn't wake up easily once she was asleep.

I kissed Luca's forehead and followed Mason out to the

living room. We both stopped in awkward silence, unsure of how to talk to each other.

"Do you want popcorn?"

"There's a game on tonight," we both started talking at the same time.

"Popcorn sounds great," Mason said and sat down in the middle of the couch, not leaving me much room on either side. I guess I was going to have to sit in the poop chair. The name was not just a name but described exactly what had happened on it. Nora wanted to get rid of it but hadn't had a chance yet.

I made the popcorn and poured it into a bowl. Mason was flicking through the channels when I got back. I put the popcorn on the table and gave the chair a look. After a slight hesitation, I perched on the edge. It was uncomfortable, and despite knowing that the chair had been scrubbed to within an inch of its life, I still didn't want to sit on it. The only one who was ever game enough to do so was Willa.

But I didn't know where Mason and I stood after the awkward and mortifying conversation this morning. And being close to him but not touching him would be torture.

Mason shot me a look that I couldn't decipher but didn't say anything about my awkward crouch. We spent a few hours making polite conversation. When we talked at all. It was awkward and made my heart ache.

I stayed in the exact same spot, until I heard the front door open, and Nora walked inside. She looked from me to Mason, and I could tell she wanted to hold back a grin but didn't quite succeed.

We said good night to Nora, who shot me a wide-eyed look that meant we would talk about this later, then drove back to his house in silence.

"Thanks for the lift," I said, walking into the house

ahead of Mason. I was tired, cranky, and my back hurt from the awkward position I had forced it in tonight.

"We both live here. No need to thank me for something that didn't require any effort on my part," he said and walked to the kitchen.

"I was just trying to be polite," I mumbled and went straight to the stairs. I needed to put a closed door between myself and Mason.

I stopped at the bottom of the stairs and took a deep breath. Guess this was it.

Before I took the first step, familiar arms lifted me and I was slung over Mason's shoulder.

"We're sorting this out right now. Because whatever you made up in your head isn't working for me," he grumbled and carried me all the way up to his bedroom.

He deposited me on his bed, where I bounced, a squeak escaping me.

I looked at him with wide eyes, too stunned to move. "What are you doing?"

"Getting you to talk to me," he said, sitting down on the bed and removing his boots.

He shuffled up until he was sitting next to my feet and our eyes met.

"It's late. I'm tired," I tried and moved to the side.

He wasn't having it, grabbing my feet and placing them in his lap. The move sent me sprawling on my back.

"What is happen—"

His fingers dug into the soles of my feet and my body relaxed and I moaned. Massages were my kryptonite.

"How did you know?" I asked. There was no way he just decided to give me a massage. He had to have known.

"Willa," he said, moving to the arch of my food. I knew he had skilled hands but this was another level. *Holy mother of God, I was dead. Dead and gone to heaven, because I could hear the angels sing their sweet melodies and strum their harps.*

I couldn't even be mad at Willa for telling him. I was too content in that moment. When I was near purring, he seized his opportunity.

"We're not going to be friends with benefits. It's a ridiculous concept that only works if neither of the people involved has feelings for the other. And there are already feelings involved, whether you like to admit it or not," he said.

I watched his serious expression and had to agree. Feelings were definitely involved. But I just didn't think it was a good idea to try anything more permanent. He was my boss. And I really needed my job. What if we broke up in a few days and I'd find myself without an income? And that was just one of the reasons why we weren't going to work.

I couldn't ever go back home. But if I had no way to support myself, I might have to. And that just wasn't an option. My fear over ending up back at home won out and I shook my head.

"It's not a good idea. What if we don't work out?"

"It's okay to take a chance in life. Especially if something great could come of it," he said, his fingers continuing to work their magic.

"Not if the risk is too great," I whispered, sadness tinging my voice.

"Then just give me tonight," Mason said.

I sat up, regretfully pulling my feet away from his hands. "I'm tired and grumpy. I won't be good company."

Another night with Mason wasn't a good idea. I was already half in love with him. Spending more time finding out how much I liked him and the spark between us might just change my mind. Which would end in disaster.

"We'll just sleep," he said, his voice having lost some of

its usual confidence. "I'm not ready to just let you walk away. I need more. Take a chance on us."

I already felt my walls crumbling. I felt safe and protected with him and sleeping one last night in his arms sounded like the sweetest temptation and worst torture.

But for once, I followed my heart and not my brain. "Okay, I guess I could do tonight."

His blinding smile made my heart twist and I almost leaned in and kissed him. I felt my resolve crumbling, no matter how much I tried putting it back together.

Five minutes later I found myself wrapped up in Mason, only wearing my panties and his shirt since he'd refused to let me go downstairs to get my pj's.

I settle against him with a contented sigh and promptly fell asleep.

14

I was nervous. So nervous that I had to reapply my lipstick twice already because I'd chewed it off. I was wearing the dress my mother had sent to the garage while I was working. It was a boring grey with capped sleeves and came down to my ankles. The shoes that accompanied it were enclosed black heels. I hated both on sight. But not wearing either wasn't an option.

My hair was up in a chignon, something I had mastered early on, since my mother insisted on me doing my mass of hair this way. It wasn't only long and thick, it was also wavy and didn't like being told what to do. Any updo required copious amounts of hairpins and a lot of cursing.

But since this wasn't my first dinner party, I was able to get myself together in about an hour. And now I was wasting time staring at myself in the bathroom mirror. I'd been standing in the same spot for the last ten minutes, wondering if this was the beginning of the end of my freedom.

And that was something I just couldn't accept. I couldn't live with my mother again. I would rather be homeless than move back into her mansion. My mother had made sure that I was unable to get a job anywhere in Humptulips but at her office. The amount of pull she had over the town sickened me.

My only saving grace had been Willa and the Drake brothers. None of them were impressed by someone throwing their money and power around and had defied her by giving me a job.

Despite my worry about tonight, my thoughts kept drifting to Mason. When we woke up this morning, I was splayed over his chest, holding onto him like he was the last available door to hang on to on the Titanic. One of his hands was on my back, holding me in place, the other was buried in my hair.

I had never cuddled with someone all night. I didn't think I would like it. But I guess Mason was good at showing me how different life could be, if I just let go of some of the control I cherished so much.

When I tried to move off him, his arms tightened around me.

"Where do you think you're going?" he had asked in a voice raspy from sleep. I was ready to melt, and he hadn't even done more than talk to me. This was getting out of hand.

"Bathroom?" I asked more than stated, since I didn't really have to go.

"I locked the door to the bedroom and hid the key. So, if I let you go to the bathroom, the easiest thing for you to do would be to come straight back to bed."

Now someone normal would have been freaked out by this. But since I was anything but normal and this might have been the last time I got to be with him like this, I found the gesture oddly romantic.

"Got it. Bathroom, then back to bed."

I lifted my head and found Mason grinning at me. His hair was all over the place and I resisted the urge to smooth it down just to feel the soft strands glide through my hand; in that moment he looked like my every dream come true.

I felt his eyes trail me to the bathroom. I quickly used the facilities and washed my hands, taking my time brushing out my hair with my fingers and swiping some toothpaste across my teeth.

I had been nervous walking back, hoping I read the signs right.

Mason lifted the covers for me to slip back under and pulled me back into him. We were facing each other, our noses nearly touching. He entangled his legs with mine and shuffled closer, bringing our fronts flush together.

"So here is what's going to happen," he started while trailing a hand up my side. "We're going to explore this thing between us." His fingers were wandering higher, brushing hair off my face in a gesture so tender I had to swallow the sudden lump in my throat.

He traced a finger across my cheekbone and lips, making me shiver. He replaced his finger with his lips, talking in between kisses.

"This thing between us is not something we can just ignore." He paused for another kiss, this one on the corner of my mouth. "We're not seeing other people. And you'll stay at my house."

I had started to protest, but he silenced me with another kiss, this time tracing my lips with his tongue. I fell silent, my breathing speeding up.

"You'll tell me what I can do to help you. I don't expect you to trust me right away, but I want to know what happened with your mother, and I want to do my part. I want us to be two parts of a whole."

God yes, I wanted that as well. I didn't know what that warm feeling in my chest was, but I figured for once my body wholeheartedly agreed with my mind. All my worries found themselves stuffed into a box and thrown into a dark basement.

He kissed my upper lip, then my lower before he started talking again. "We're going to be late for work today. I hope that's okay."

I had nearly laughed but instead told him, "You're the boss. And if nothing else I try to be a good employee and follow directions."

"Excellent. Then as your boss, I'll tell you to touch me."

He had barely finished talking when my hands were making their way in between our bodies, tracing his glorious abs. I explored to my heart's content, enjoying the feel of his chiseled body. His back muscles contracted when I ran a hand over them. I did it again, just because I could.

He was only wearing boxers, and I sneaked my hand into the back, then let it wander to the front. Mason wasn't a silent participant; instead, he kissed me deep, while his hands made my body sing.

When I thought I couldn't wait any longer, and Mason had pushed me to the brink only to bring me back again and again, he reached behind him into the nightstand. I nearly wept when I heard the crinkle of foil.

We had stayed on our sides, facing each other, one of my legs up over his hip. He entered me slowly, giving me time to adjust. Once he was fully seated inside, I sighed in pleasure. He started moving and I arched my head back, unable to contain a moan. He went slow and gentle, our movements speaking of our feelings for each other.

I had really been kidding myself when I thought I

could just walk away from this. It was already so much more than I could have ever imagined.

My head came back and he captured my gaze with his eyes that were full of tenderness and passion. It didn't take me long to fall over the edge. Mason wasn't far behind, his thrusts coming faster before he finished with one long groan.

He kissed me again and again, our bodies still connected. When he pulled away, I groaned in protest and he chuckled.

"I'll be back, beautiful. Don't go anywhere."

I flopped on my back and imitated a starfish. "Couldn't even if I wanted to."

We spent the early morning hours in bed, talking and kissing. We kept the topics light and the kisses heavy. It was something else I would never forget. A feeling of joy so strong I was bursting with it.

We finally made it into work around eleven, but I could have stayed in bed all day. It felt like nothing else in the world existed but the two of us.

The morning was such a contrast to where I stood now. Any happiness I had felt was gone. My usually vibrant dark green eyes looked dull and the angles of my face harsh, thanks to the tight chignon I had wrestled my hair into. Reality had me in its grip once again, and I wondered what the hell I'd been thinking.

One touch and I forgot all the reasons why I should stay away from Mason.

But for now my only worry was tonight. It was the last official party before the election. I knew my mother would force me to stand next to her on Election Day. But after that, I doubted she would care what I was doing or with whom. At least that's what I hoped.

I grabbed my lipstick and powder and dropped them

in the black clutch that looked just as boring as the rest of my outfit. After fiddling with the clasp for longer than necessary, I finally left the bathroom and collided with Mason.

"Sorry," I said and stepped to the side.

"Where are you going?" he asked, sweeping a look at my outfit with raised brows.

"Out."

"Right. I can see that. Out where?"

"Just dinner."

A look at my watch confirmed that it was almost eight and I was running late.

"How come you haven't mentioned this before now?"

He followed me down the stairs, his presence a comfort that I couldn't allow myself to enjoy for long. I had a persona to put on and people to impress.

"I forgot all about it." *Or more like refused to think about tonight.* "It's just a thing at my mother's."

We made it to the hallway and he stepped in front of me. "You're not going there alone."

I blinked at the harshness in his voice. I had gotten used to the gentle version of him, and his tone took me by surprise.

"I usually show up by myself. No way would I subject anyone else to her presence."

"Too bad then, since I'm coming with you."

I tripped, and he caught me with a hand on my waist. "You what?"

He let me go and grabbed a coat off a hook by the door. "You heard me."

"You can't—" A horn beeping outside interrupted me.

He took my hand and pressed a kiss to my palm before interlacing his fingers with mine. "I presume that's our ride. Let's go, beautiful."

I was too stunned to protest when he led me outside and down the porch stairs. A driver was holding open the back door of a black town car.

We both got in, Mason sitting next to me, still holding my hand.

"You have no idea what you're getting yourself into," I warned.

He placed a kiss on top of my head. "I can handle it."

We made the short drive in silence, and when we pulled up to the gate at the entrance to my mother's farm, Mason whistled. "This is where you grew up?"

"Unfortunately," I couldn't help but answer.

The gate was open and the long driveway was lined with cars. My mother had valet services for nights like tonight, and the whole dinner was planned to within an inch of its short life.

We stopped in front of the ostentatious fountain that every McMansion seemed to require. The thing served no purpose but to take up a lot of space in the middle of the curved driveway and waste thousands of gallons of water.

Our door opened, and a valet held out his hand to help me out of the car. "Ma'am."

Mason didn't let me take the offered hand; instead, he got out first and shooed the valet away. He then helped me out of the car, and once I was standing outside, he placed my hand in the crook of his arm.

Music was drifting through the air, the piano playing a familiar tune. The Connors liked tradition. Boring tradition, but tradition nonetheless. Nothing ever changed at these events. Even the napkins were exactly the same, which made this worse because I knew what was coming.

I bit my lip again, already resigned to the fact that I would have to reapply my lipstick a few times tonight.

What the hell was I even doing here? This wasn't me anymore. And it never had been.

Mason put his hand on mine. "Come on, princess, let's get this over with."

"Yeah, let's," I answered and closed my fingers around his arm even tighter. His presence was like an anchor, stopping me from floating away amongst the fake tans and polished diamonds I'd be looking at once inside.

Mason wasn't dressed for an elegant dinner, but I couldn't care less. I loved him in his jeans and a T-shirt, especially when it was his favorite Ramones shirt that fit tight over his chest and arms.

But if I knew one thing about Mason, it was that he had unwavering self-confidence. He was unapologetic about who he was and what he wanted. If I had to pick anyone to come with me tonight, it would have been him.

"Fuck me, this place is a castle," Mason said as soon as we stepped inside. And the only thing he could see so far was the entry hall. It was huge—a waste of space really—and it was tacky. But it was also impressive, thanks to the abundance of marble, gold, and mahogany.

"It wears off quickly."

Especially since living here came with a set of iron rules.

"Right," he chuckled. "So where to?"

I tugged on his arm, and he followed me through a door to the right. The best thing would be to let go of him. There was no way my mother would be okay with Mason being here—and it was becoming impossible for me to walk even a step without touching him. She'd know what he meant to me as soon as she saw us, but I just couldn't get myself to put space between Mason and me.

"Dinner is served in the dining hall." I pointed to a door at the other end of the grand ballroom. "This is the room we have to get through so we can sit down and pretend to love the food and not talk to anyone."

Mason walked a few steps inside and looked around the vast space. It was filled with people, but they did nothing to distract from the crystal chandeliers, gilded mirrors, and velvet curtains. If anything, the expensive gowns most of the women wore only complemented the designs of the room. I wondered what Mason thought of all this excess.

"Well, that's a lot of gold. Guess if you ever run out of money, you can just start melting candle holders and mirror frames," he remarked.

I smiled, thinking I could get through tonight as long as he was there. I was trying to figure out how to best make my way across the room undetected, when I heard a voice that froze me.

"Darling, so glad you made it."

I was pulled away from Mason and into the arms of my stepfather. I swallowed a mouth full of his hair when I tried to gasp for breath. He squeezed me hard, and I nearly drowned in the cloud of aftershave that always followed him wherever he went.

"Aren't you going to introduce me to your date?" he asked, not letting go of my hand.

I hated when he touched me. He had tried kissing me a few times before I moved out. If you had boobs, he would hit on you. But he was always discreet with his affairs and devoted to my mother's career—the only thing she cared about—so she let him do what he wanted.

He appraised Mason with a narrowed gaze and a once-over.

"Mason, this is Leighton—" I started but was cut off by my mother, who was now beside her husband.

"I hope this isn't your date," she murmured, not

looking at me. Her eyes were on Mason, and it was clear that she found him lacking.

"Hello, mother. May I introduce you to Mason Drake."

Neither Mason nor my mother made any move to shake hands or acknowledge each other with anything else than disapproving glares.

"He needs to go. Now," my mother said, her voice tightly controlled. She didn't want anyone to overhear our conversation, but I knew she was angry when I saw her hands tapping her thighs in rapid succession.

"If you want me to stay, then so will Mason."

"Ungrateful brat. You truly are my biggest mistake," she muttered. Not the first time she'd slung an insult like this one at me. I barely flinched.

She turned around and stalked away, dragging her husband with her.

Mason turned to me and studied my face. "You okay?" he asked, his voice heavy with concern.

"I'm fine. It's nothing I haven't heard before."

I might have expected my mother to be a bitch tonight, but that didn't mean it hurt any less. My armor of choice was sarcastic comments and jokes. But I had nothing at the moment, feeling deflated and embarrassed Mason heard her comments.

"I'm sorry she was rude to you," I said, studying my toes.

Mason turned to face me and lifted my chin up. "Don't you dare apologize for her. And I wasn't really the one she insulted. You deserve so much better than this. I hope you know that."

I looked at him and realized he really meant what he just said. I put my hand on his chest and leaned closer. "I'm sorry you got dragged into this. Things are likely to get worse from here."

"How's the food at these things?" Mason asked.

"Terrible. Unless you like unpronounceable, tiny dishes."

Mason winked at me. "Let's live a little and eat at least three mystery dishes."

I felt the corners of my mouth lift into a smile. "You're on. Just don't come crying to me afterward when you have intestines stuck in your teeth."

"Do I want to know?"

I scrunched up my nose. "It's a French specialty. Just don't eat anything that sounds like *Andouillette*. Even if you think the waiter said baguette."

"Noted." He waved to a passing waiter. "Drink?" he asked and lifted two glasses off the tray before I could respond.

"Thanks," I said and gratefully took the champagne he held out.

We almost made it to the other end of the room before someone stopped us again. And to think we were so close to the salvation of the dining room.

"Stella, sweetheart, how are you? It's been ages," a sickly-sweet voice stopped me. I tightened my hand holding the glass to stop it from slipping. Throwing precious alcohol on people was not the solution.

"Charlotte, it hasn't been long enough," I responded and grimaced at her, making sure to show all my teeth. I found that acting like you had a few cups missing usually got you out of uncomfortable situations quickly.

"And who is this interesting young man you brought with you today?"

"This is Mason. He's my sponsor."

Mason coughed next to me and squeezed my hand.

Charlotte's smile didn't slip. Probably because she had so much Botox in her face, it was hard to change facial

137

expressions in under a minute. That was if she managed to at all.

"Well, he sure is something." She held her hand out to Mason like she expected him to kiss it. I was ready to slap her hand away and just leave when Mason leaned into her.

"I'm sorry, but I'm not supposed to touch people. Part of my parole," he whispered. It was my turn to cough and struggle to hold back the laughter.

"Is that Judy? I think it is. I better go and say hello," Charlotte stuttered and left in a cloud of Clive Christian No. 1.

Good riddance. Too bad that she was the biggest gossip and soon the whole room would think I was an addict and Mason an ex-con. But I didn't really care, since getting rid of her quicker than I had ever managed before was worth it.

"I can see why you like hanging around these people. They're charming," Mason remarked and stopped another waiter, this time for the tray of food he was carrying. "Does the name of this sound even remotely like baguette?" he asked and pointed to the little squares on the plate.

The waiter didn't miss a beat and shook his head. "No, sir. These are caviar bites."

"Sounds safe enough to me," Mason said and grabbed three off the plate. He put all of them in his mouth at the same time, but as soon as he started to chew his face went slack. He looked around wide-eyed, and I turned to the waiter.

"Can I borrow that serviette over your arm, please?"

The waiter handed it over without complaint, and I passed it to Mason who buried his head inside. He emerged shortly after and rolled the serviette together.

"That was the most disgusting thing I've ever put in

my mouth. And I've swallowed oil before." He wiped his tongue with the side of the napkin that wasn't rolled up. "You could have warned me."

"How would I know you don't like caviar. People seem to love it."

"So, where to next?" he asked and took my hand again. The gesture felt natural and I loved the contact.

"Let's hide in the dining room until they serve dinner. We'll have to sit through a few speeches before they serve the food, then we can make a quick getaway."

He nodded and we swerved around guests as we walked to the other end of the room. The door was open and a few guests had already made their way inside. Rows of tables lined the front of a stage, each table adorned with nametags.

The seating plan was a masterpiece in itself, every person placed strategically around the room. Because God forbid someone sat next to a person they could actually have an intelligent conversation with. The only topic anyone would be talking about tonight was the campaign.

My mother was a master at networking and manipulation. I knew how these things worked, having sat through many identical dinners.

I found my name on a table close to the stage and cringed. One of my mother's closest supporters was allocated the seat next to mine.

David had just come back from D.C. His political ambitions rivaled my mother's and they supported each other with their campaigns. He had come back to make sure my mother won. In turn she would be in DC for his next campaign. They both wanted to get into the senate, and my mother had the money and David the connections.

Leighton was seated on my other side. I stole a name

tag off the table next to us and turned it over and wrote Mason's name on it.

I balled up David's name tag and threw it under the table and put my newly created one in its place. Mason watched me, silently taking in the decorations.

"Just when I thought I've seen it all, I walk into a house that has a room with an actual stage," he murmured.

"Yeah, that was an addition my mother made a few years ago." I cringed at what Mason must think of my family.

We took our seats and watched more and more people trickle inside. A bell rang soon after we sat down, signaling the start of the speeches. My mother appeared on the side of the stage, Leighton and David behind her.

Her advisor, Leon, was handing her his notes while running a fluff roller over her suit. My cousin Zeke was standing off to the side talking on his phone. I knew my uncle and aunt were here somewhere as well, as was my other cousin Rosie, Zeke's sister.

It felt like Groundhog Day, her routine the same every single time. I also knew all the speeches, as did most of the people here tonight. But I guess they weren't here to listen to her talk but to show their support.

"Ma'am, you're needed at the podium," one of my mother's lackeys who was standing behind my chair said.

I was biting my lip, the only sign that I was anything but calm. I took my time getting up, making sure to smooth out non-existent wrinkles once I was standing.

I locked eyes with Mason who was watching me, looking ready to take me away if I said the word. But I wouldn't ever ask that of him. I'd already painted a big enough target on his back.

I put a hand on his shoulder. "This shouldn't take long."

Before he had a chance to respond, I walked to the stage. I joined the group and lifted my chin. I only had to do this one more time, and I could wash my hands of this farce.

My mother didn't acknowledge me, neither did Zeke. But since my cousin and I had been at odds since we were kids, it wasn't surprising.

We followed a composed Clementine Connor onto the stage and took our assigned places. We had done this so many times before, that nobody faltered; it looked like a choreographed performance.

My mother started her speech and I tuned out, the only way to stay awake during these things. I had once nodded off, not having slept well the night before. The wrath that rained down on me from that little slipup was one I would never forget. Lucky for me, we weren't sitting down this time so there was no chance of my eyes closing. At least I hoped not.

I looked up when a murmur went through the room and noticed everyone was staring at me, including my mother.

"Stella, are you coming?" she prompted, and I looked at her outstretched hand, realizing she wanted me to join her. That one was new. It made my stomach clench and bile rose in my throat. Changing the script this late in the campaign didn't bode well for me.

David appeared by my side and took my arm, escorting me to the front of the stage. The strangeness continued when my mother smiled at me and put her arm around my shoulders. *What. The. Hell.*

"Here they are," my mother said, and I watched her, confused as to where this was going.

She was still smiling her fake smile. "As many of you know, my daughter and David are friends. They have always had a special bond, and since he has come back to town, their romance has rekindled. I'm proud to officially welcome David to our family." My eyes went wide, and I was sure they were going to pop out of my head. Unless my head was going to explode first.

I tried to step away from my mother and David, but his hold was unrelenting. "May I introduce to you the future Mrs. Sterling," my mother announced, finally letting me go, only for me to end up in a tight hug from David.

My heart dropped and my mouth went dry. What the hell indeed? Was he out of his mind?

"Just go with it," David whispered into my ear before he kissed me. He was lucky I was stunned speechless and immobile, or I would have kicked him in the balls right after I bit off his tongue that sneaked out.

I leaned back and he released his hold on me. It was all about keeping up appearances after all, and a struggle by the newly engaged couple wouldn't look too great to voters.

There was applause, and then we were finally allowed to get off the stage. David tried to talk to me, but I held up my hand, stopping his fumbled explanations. We were standing next to the stage and people were still looking so slapping him was out of the question.

"This is insane. Fuck you for going along with this. I thought you were better than her," I hissed and walked away, leaving a flustered David behind.

I made it to the table and hoped Mason was ready to get out of there. No way was I going to stay another minute. But when I looked at the seat he was supposed to be sitting in, it was empty. And there was no sign of Mason.

15

"Get back to your seat. Now," my mother hissed while waving to someone.

I was still stunned from what had just happened on stage. And where did Mason go?

"I'm not going to say it again," my mother's voice jolted me out of my dazed state.

For lack of a better idea, I did as I was told and sat down. Who knew how much longer my feet were going to keep me up anyway. I should never have obeyed and attended this fiasco.

David dropped into the seat next to me and took my hand.

"I know you don't understand what's going on, but I couldn't tell you before the announcement. It was your mother's decision, and I agreed that this was best for the campaign. Just don't make a scene, and we can talk about it tonight after everyone leaves."

I pulled my hand back and he let go when he realized I wasn't going to back down. "You are out of your mind if you think I'm going to talk to you. And I'll gladly repeat myself so you understand where I stand. This is insane."

I didn't touch any of the food that was brought out and refused to participate in the conversation around the table. Leighton tried to get me to talk to him, but I just ignored whatever he was saying. I was good at tuning people out and he was easy to ignore. He eventually got the hint and gave up.

I texted Mason to find out where he was, but he didn't reply. I texted again. There was still no reply.

As soon as dinner was finished, I jumped up. Time to get out of there. A guy I hadn't met before stopped me when I turned from the table.

"Excuse me," I said and tried to walk past him. He matched my movements and shook his head.

"Ma'am, you're supposed to stay here."

"Yeah, well, and my mother is supposed to care about me. We can't always get what we want." I made another attempt at walking past him and was thwarted again. Seriously, what was it with these brainless thugs my mother seemed to be hiring lately?

"Let me through," I ground out.

"Stella. Cease this behavior at once," my mother admonished.

"What behavior? Trying to go home?"

"You are home. But I see you need a reminder of proper etiquette. Tomorrow we will pick your lessons back up where we left off before your little tantrum."

My blood ran cold and my whole body went still.

"I'm not staying here."

"Oh, but you are. Just think of your friend and her kids."

Just the mention of Nora made all my resistance evaporate. She knew how to get my compliance.

"Fine. Now, if you'll excuse me," I clipped, storming out.

This was a nightmare I wish I could wake up from. Nobody stopped me, but I noticed the hired muscle followed me up to my room.

I slammed the door behind me, at least as much as one could slam a heavy oak door, and took in my room.

It looked exactly how I left it. A lot of soft pink and white, and a hideous wallpaper that I had hated from the moment I first saw it. I had had no hand in decorating the room and wasn't allowed to change anything once the interior designer was finished. I was a stranger in my own home, careful of every step I took and every word I said.

It was exhausting. And now I was right back to where I started. I had to get out before things escalated. That was one thing I was sure about. My mother wouldn't just let me get away with my defiance. She was good at biding her time and waiting for the right moment to put me back in my place. I felt pathetic, letting my mother control me like that.

My eyes closed for only a moment before I was jostled awake by a knock on my door. I sat up, disoriented and still in the same clothes. I tried to turn on my phone to check the time, but it was dead. It was getting light outside which told me I must have slept all night.

The knock sounded again, and I got up and opened the door only to come face to face with David. My eyes narrowed, and I suppressed the urge to snarl at him. Instead, I closed the door on him without a word.

"Stella, come on. Don't be like that. We need to talk."

I glared at the door. "Nothing to talk about, other than you're a backstabbing, heartless minion."

"Now that's a bit harsh, don't you think? I understand you're angry, but you'll come to see the value of this connection as soon as you calm down."

"The only people benefitting from this arrangement are

you and my mother. Not sure how you could think this is anything I would ever accept."

He was delusional. Surely, he would understand how this ridiculous idea would never go anywhere.

"Don't you want to get out from under your mother's thumb? If you marry me, you'll have all the freedom you ever wanted."

That thought made me stop pacing and stare at the door. I had a taste of freedom and wanted to keep it. The thought of having to go back to the way things were made me nauseous.

But the thought of marrying David felt wrong. Not while I had such strong feelings for Mason.

Five minutes of silence passed and I thought he'd left.

"If you open the door, we can talk about this like the mature adults we are. I know you'll come to see how this is going to benefit you as well."

I didn't make a move to open the door. I needed time to think and come up with a way to get out of this mess. And I had to talk to Willa.

A business card was pushed under my door. "That's my new number. Call me when you're ready to talk."

His receding footsteps meant that I was finally alone. I went back to the bed and searched the nightstand for a charger. I didn't have much luck and gave up in defeat.

I got a change of clothes out of my still-overflowing closet and turned on the water in my bathroom. It was as big as Willa's living room, the rainfall shower something I had to admit I missed.

I stripped my clothes off and stepped into the warm water. It was heaven standing under the stream, and for the first time my arm didn't sting when it got wet. At least I was almost back to normal.

After a long shower, I dressed back in jeans that were

hidden in the back of my closet and a blouse. Wearing jeans was a statement I wanted to make, since they were something that I was never allowed to wear.

I slipped into a pair of flats and made my way down to the kitchen. Only Maria, our housekeeper, was there and she let out an excited yelp when she saw it was me.

"*Mija*, you are back," she said in her heavily accented English.

She had always been one of my favorite people, having worked here for as long as I could remember. She also secretly taught me a few words of Spanish even though I wasn't allowed to learn any per my mother's decree.

Once my dad was gone, she forbade any reminders he ever existed and that included the language.

I stepped into Maria's embrace, and a few tears rolled down my cheeks. She was like a surrogate mom, always looking out for me and being my sounding board when I needed it.

"I missed you," I sniffed into her starched blouse, taking in the familiar scent of laundry detergent and food.

"*Mi corazón*," she whispered and petted my back.

After a few minutes, I let go and wiped my eyes with the tissue she handed me.

"I'm happy to see you, but why are you back?" she asked.

"Mother made me."

She shook her head and got a cup out and filled it with coffee. "That woman," she said.

That was as far as she would ever go with showing her displeasure. I knew she was worked up when she didn't say anything else. Maria always chose her words carefully and never spoke in anger. It wasn't her way and something I wish I learned from her. Not that she didn't try to teach me how to control my impulsiveness, but my temper usually got the best of me.

She held the coffee out to me and I gratefully took it. "*Gracias*," I whispered, still too much of that frightened little girl in me to speak any language other than English in this house too loudly.

"Do you have a phone charger by any chance?" I asked and held up my phone. She nodded and went to rummage through a drawer.

I plugged my phone in and continued to sip my coffee. Maria hustled around the kitchen, getting lunch organized, most likely. Mealtimes had to be carefully planned out, and my mother didn't allow for anyone to be late or for a meal to be anything but what she had planned for the week.

I turned my phone back on, and it beeped a few times but otherwise stayed silent. I had a message from Willa, who was checking in, and one from Rayna, telling me she was trialing a new donut flavor and needed a taste tester.

It was nearly nine, and if I didn't get my butt into gear, I was going to be late for work. Where I still intended to go, since all my mother had asked of me was to move back in, not to stay in the house all day. I knew it's what she implied, but she couldn't punish me for something that she didn't outright order me to do.

I would sleep here for now, to make sure Nora and the kids were fine. But I had every intention of coming up with a plan to cut my ties to her once and for all.

Maria drove me to work since she had to go into town anyway. She parked in front of Drake's Garage and looked at me with sad eyes.

"Thanks for driving me. I'll get my car and drive myself back tonight," I said.

"Don't be late for dinner. You know how she gets."

And did I ever. I would make sure to be there on time. "I haven't forgotten."

She gave me one last sorrowful look; I knew she wanted better for me. And I wanted better for me, but that wasn't something I could change at the moment. I had to concentrate on the things I could control. Like getting my butt inside, so I wouldn't lose my only source of income and way out of here.

Because if there was one thing last night had shown me, it was the only person I could rely on was myself. And I had to make sure I had enough money behind me to finally leave this town behind.

The office was quiet, the only noise the hustle and bustle from the workshop. I had to talk to Mason, but as soon as I sat down at my desk, the phone rang and didn't stop until it was past lunch.

I was starving and made myself a sandwich from the meager supplies. There was an old fridge in the kitchen where the guys kept their lunch and usually a few things to make a sandwich. But it looked like it hadn't been stocked in a while.

I texted Willa while I waited for the newly fixed coffee machine to heat up.

Me: *Code Red. Call me.*

The big machine was amazing, but so complicated I usually made myself an espresso instead of a cappuccino. I'd also broken it twice already, but lucky for me, the repair guy was a good customer and didn't charge us to fix it.

When I was finished making my sandwich, Willa still

hadn't responded. I took a bite and nearly spat it back out. It tasted like sawdust and I grimaced. But then again, what did I expect from stale bread and old ham. There was no butter, and we were out of cheese.

I threw it in the garbage after a few bites, not hungry enough to choke it down. I didn't want to wait any longer to talk to Mason. I was hurt he hadn't come to the office to speak to me. I needed to know why he left last night.

The guys were all working on cars, the music was blaring and Landon was shaking his hips to the beat. I smiled at his bad dancing and stopped in front of Mason's bay. He was bent over a motorbike, his overalls rolled down to his waist, his muscular arms on full display.

I stared for a few seconds, hoping he would hear me out. Seeing me kiss another man was probably the nail in the coffin of our short relationship. But I had to try to make things right.

"Mason," I called over the music.

He looked up and his eyes were as cold as ice. His face didn't give anything away. The only indication that he wasn't altogether unaffected by my appearance was the tight grip he had on his wrench and the tick in his jaw.

He didn't say anything, just looked at me, his gaze growing angrier the longer I stood there.

"Why—" I started and had to clear my throat when my voice was breaking. "Why did you leave last night?"

"Really, Stella?"

"What do you mean? I thought we were at least friends. And friends don't leave each other behind."

"You seemed just fine up on that stage. I'm sure your fiancé could have taken you home," he spat, turning back to the bike he was working on.

"It's not what it looked like."

He turned his head. "You are delusional if you think I'll

buy that line. You looked right at home on that stage, and I didn't exactly see you put up a fight when he kissed you."

"If you'd just let me explain—"

"Explain what? How you let another guy kiss you the same day you woke up in my bed? How you pretended to hate having to go to the dinner party, but once you were there you were all smiles and queenly waves?"

Now it was my turn to get mad, and as usual, my temper got the best of me. "I didn't want him to kiss me and I knew nothing of an engagement," I yelled. "What the hell is your problem?"

"My problem? My fucking problem," he roared, his voice carrying loud enough over the music that Landon and Clay poked their heads up, "is that you are a spoiled little princess who thinks she can use everyone as if they don't matter. My problem is that you play the victim card so well, when in reality, it was a game to you all along. My problem, princess, is *you*."

I stumbled back, stunned by his anger. I understood that the kiss might have seemed like more than what it was, but he just needed to listen to me. Helpless to stop the tears from streaming down my face, I wiped at them furiously.

"Stop calling me that," I whispered. He must have heard me because he turned toward me again, delivering his last blow.

"Since this is where we part ways, that won't be a problem."

"Are you firing me?"

"Isn't it obvious?"

"You can't fire me," I said, stumbling over the words.

He laughed a humorless laugh. "Watch me."

With that, he turned his back on me and continued working on the motorbike in his bay.

A loud sob escaped me, but I slapped my hand over my mouth. This was what I had been trying to avoid. But because I'd been unable to stay away from him, I'd not only lost Mason but also my job.

Landon stepped forward and put his arm around me.

"Come on, sugar pie, let the fire-breathing dragon stew in his own misery," he said and led me out of the workshop.

He walked me through the office and I grabbed my things, unable to process what just happened. *Way to go, Stella, losing Mason and your job all in one day. You always were an overachiever.*

"Can you take me to get my car?"

"Of course, just let me grab my keys and we can get out of here."

He made good on his word and was back a few seconds later. We silently made our way to his Dodge Charger and got in. The engine purred to life, and we shot out of the parking lot. My breath hitched and I held onto the seat, hoping this car had airbags. Because I was pretty sure I was going to die if it didn't.

"He didn't mean it," Landon said. I was too petrified to take my eyes off the road, so I talked to him, keeping my eyes forward.

"I'm pretty sure he did."

"He has a short temper. Give him a few hours and he'll regret being such a dick."

"Right. So, it's okay that he just treated me like I was less than the oil stain on the floor of his work bay?"

Landon put a hand on my arm, which almost caused me to look over to him. "Put your hand back on the steering wheel," I told the windscreen instead. Mercifully he took his hand back.

"Of course, it's not. I just don't want you to give up on him. He's a good guy."

"He can't just treat people like they're disposable."

Landon sighed and turned into the street Willa's apartment was on. "I know, sugarplum. But don't take it personal. He has some trust issues. And whatever happened between you two must have really hurt him for him to lash out like that."

"Landon, I know you're his friend and therefore feel required to defend him, but sometimes people don't need a reason for the things they do. I lived with a lunatic control freak for most of my life, and she certainly had no good reason for the things she did. I'm done making excuses, let alone accepting shitty explanations."

Landon parked the car outside the apartment. "Stella, just don't...."

I opened the door, shaking my head. "Stop, Landon. I'm done."

He looked at his lap and sighed. "Okay. I get it. But please think about coming back tomorrow. I promise you, he'll feel like shit about what he said to you."

I didn't answer just got out and closed the door. Landon was still parked outside when I went up the flight of stairs to my apartment. I only heard the noise of his car engine fade once I was safely inside.

I don't know if it was the snot running down my face, thanks to a ten-minute crying jag, or the vodka I had gulped down as soon as I was inside the apartment, but it was like a light came on and I saw clearly what I had to do.

I packed all my things that were still spread around Willa's place and got my phone out. For some insane reason, the business card David had pushed under the door was tucked into my purse, something I did before leaving my room that morning.

It felt foolish at the time, but now I was glad I did it.

I dialed his number and he picked up after a few short rings.

"David Sterling."

"David, it's Stella."

"I was hoping you'd call," he said, unable to hide the surprise in his voice.

I took a deep breath. This was it. There was no way out after this. "I'll do it."

"That's fantastic. You won't regret it. I promise," he rushed to say.

"I have a few conditions before we make it official."

"Of course. I wouldn't have expected anything less from a Connor."

I shoved the rest of my things into my handbag and glanced around the apartment, making sure I didn't miss anything. The lump in my throat threatened to choke off my air. I wasn't sure I was doing the right thing, but at this moment, it was the only thing I could do.

I wasn't going back to my mother's, and the only way she would leave Nora alone was if I went along with her plans to marry David.

It would be fine. Everything would be fine. It was just marriage. People did it all the time.

16

"You sure about this?" David asked me the next morning. "This is a five-year deal. You'd be giving up a lot. But also gaining a lot."

"Yes, I'm sure," I said, not sure at all what in the world I was doing. But I hadn't come up with a better plan, and I didn't have much time before my mother would suck me back into her world.

We were standing in front of my family's front door to talk to my mother. After I talked to David, we met and drew up a contract. We agreed on most points, but this last one I had to talk David into. Because it meant that I would move in with him immediately. And we were here to tell my mother.

The door opened and the devil herself stood there. And we didn't even say her name three times.

"What an interesting surprise. Do come in, unless you plan on standing out there like you're ready to rob the place."

I didn't roll my eyes or make a snarky comeback. Someone should give me an award, because that cost me a lot of my self-control.

We followed her into her study, another larger-than-life room. The second story had been taken out to make it a two-story monstrosity that was lined with books. I doubted any of them had ever been so much as opened.

"Coffee?" she offered David, who nodded. She ignored my presence and I was glad to draw as little attention to myself as possible. We sat down, my mother in her big chair behind her desk, David and I in front of her, our chairs lower to the ground and much smaller. Everything was a power play in her world and my mother was its master.

"Talk," my mother commanded, and I leaned forward in the uncomfortable chair.

"David and I have come to an agreement."

"Did you now? And what would this agreement be?" She leaned back, knowing that she'd won.

"We'll get married, where and when you want, but I'm moving in with David today and you promise to leave my friends alone."

My mother took a sip of her own coffee and studied us. The silence stretched for a while and I was growing restless, not to mention uncomfortable in the hard chair.

"Seems like you learned something from me after all. I agree to your terms."

That seemed too easy. She never gave in like that. *Why didn't she come up with ridiculous terms? What was happening? Is this the end of the world? Are we all going to die? Does this mean I'll never get to watch the Lord of the Rings again?*

"You may get your things while David and I talk," my mother said, dismissing me from their conversation like I was a child.

Now that was more like her. But I didn't even care that she just insulted me by wanting me out of the room while the adults talked.

I got up and all but ran out of the study, grateful that I wasn't going to destroy anyone else's life today. David seemed all too happy when I told him my conditions, and he always liked working with my mother. I guess like attracted like, and those two were similar in their relentless drive to succeed.

Once I closed the office door behind me, I started running, darting up the stairs, only slowing down once I was in front of my room. I rushed inside and closed the door, leaning my back against it.

This time there was no way I would ever come back, so I had some serious packing to do. I should have packed everything the last time I moved out, since I wasn't planning on coming back then either. But that departure hadn't been a well-planned operation and more like a hastily thrown-together escape while my mother and Leighton were in Barbados.

I pushed away from the door and went into my walk-in closet. This time I got all my suitcases out and started throwing clothes and books inside. I was forced to leave half my shoes and nearly all my heavy winter coats behind. But nevertheless, I still had five big suitcases that were too heavy for me to carry. I had to look the part of a politician's wife, and the clothes I had been forced to wear all my life would be perfect for my new one.

My desperate need to get out of the house drove me to push the suitcases to the top of the stairs. I couldn't lift them up, but I might be able to push them down. The few picture frames I had weren't in any of the suitcases, so there was nothing breakable in them.

David appeared at the bottom of the stairs just as I was ready to push the first suitcase down.

"What are you doing?" he asked and came up to meet me.

"Debating how much noise it would make if I pushed them down," I answered and pointed at the suitcase.

"Good to see you haven't changed," he said, sounding anything but happy about that fact.

"Do you mind getting them down?" I asked. He nodded and lifted one suitcase in each hand. He grunted and put them back down.

"What the hell did you put in them? Furniture?"

"Not exactly. But you'll appreciate what's in them. I've been groomed my entire life for the role of a politician's wife. And the clothes in those suitcases are a part of it."

"I like that you are throwing yourself into this wholeheartedly. I think we'll make a great team," he said and started carrying them down one by one.

"Not sure how they're going to fit in my car," he grouched when he passed me on his way down for suitcase number three.

"We can stack them on the back seat if necessary," I said.

It had to work, because I wasn't coming back. Once I was gone, I had no plans on ever returning.

We made it fit somehow, and after one last glance at the ostentatious mansion I'd grown up in, I got in the car and closed the door on my old life. Hopefully for the last time.

The drive to his house took a while since he lived in the hills. At least that's what everyone dubbed them. It was a new development in the middle of nowhere and overlooked a man-made lake. He pulled into his driveway, and I parked next to him. His place was brand new and looked straight out of a catalogue.

"Don't know if I can fit all your clothes in my closet," David joked as he lugged one of my suitcases up his porch.

"We're not staying in the same room so that won't be an issue," I said and followed him to his front door.

"We'll see," he answered and walked inside. If he thought this was going to be anything more than two people helping each other out, he would be sorely disappointed.

The inside looked like it had been surgically cleaned. The smell of paint lingered in the air, and he certainly had a penchant for white, since there was barely any color in the room. It wasn't anything like the bachelor pad I expected to see.

"How long have you lived here?" I asked.

"I bought this place as soon as I got back."

"It's very clean."

He smiled at my comment and pointed at the stairs. "There's four rooms on the second floor and they all come with their own bathrooms."

We walked upstairs, leaving the suitcases near the doors for now. "The last door on the right is my room. You can pick any of the other three rooms. Take as much space as you like," David said and did something akin to a royal wave toward the rooms.

There were two rooms on each side, all spacious and light.

He showed me his bedroom after he pointed out the three guest rooms. He lied when he said he didn't think my stuff would fit in his closet, because his clothes hardly took up any room. The walk-in was enormous, and two whole sides were still empty.

"In case you change your mind," he said and nodded at the empty shelves and hanging space.

I ignored him and went back downstairs to get my suitcases. Or rather, I supervised while David carried all my possessions to one of his guestrooms.

I didn't care which one I stayed in, so when he asked where to put my stuff, I just pointed to the room on the left that was closest to the staircase and farthest away from his room.

"I'll be downstairs if you need anything," David said and left me to unpack.

The thought of getting all my stuff out made me nauseous, and instead of unpacking, I crawled under the cream comforter and pulled it over my head. Sleep sounded like a great idea.

The ringing of my phone woke me from a disturbing dream that included hairy aliens and a tennis match. I fumbled for my bag that I'd dropped on the nightstand. Before I managed to get my phone out, it stopped ringing but started up again.

I finally found it and saw it was Willa who was calling. Fucking finally.

"It's about time you called me back," I greeted her.

"Are you okay? What happened? Why are we having a code red? Are you dying? Did you finally find out what that weird spot on your arm was?"

"The spot on my arm is a birthmark, so no, I'm not going to die from it. And Mason fired me."

"He did what?" Willa yelled. "How? What? When? I don't understand. How? No, start with when. No, wait, tell me what he said first."

"He said that I was fired. And I really need you to listen to what I have to say and let me finish before you freak out."

"That doesn't sound like something I want to do. Should I get Jameson? I'm going to get Jameson."

She left to get Jameson while I waited and wondered if I should tell her the whole story.

"Okay, we're back and you're on speaker."

I groaned but made the decision to just tell her what I had done. Kind of like ripping off a Band-Aid. At least she wasn't close enough to lock me in her bedroom until I saw reason. Something she'd done to Maisie last year when she refused to apply for a special design program. It ended with a four-hour-long standoff and a filled-out application.

"Okay, so just remember to not freak out. Maybe start deep breathing now. Better to get a head start on the right technique."

"I don't like this, Estrella. I don't think you should tell me yet. Maybe don't do whatever you want to do until I come back. It's only a few more weeks."

"It's already too late for that. I signed a contract that I intend to honor. And besides, there's a penalty for not holding up my end of the deal. After you hear me out and still want to talk me out of this, save your breath. It's a done deal."

"Stop. I changed my mind. I'm coming back today."

"No, you're not. You're finally doing something for yourself. I'm fine. Things here are fine. Just let me tell you what's going on. It's not that bad. At least if you consider the alternatives."

"Are we talking Vegas bad or missing satellite dish bad?"

"Vegas bad with a few damaged satellite dishes."

I heard a squeaky inhale but knew that I had to tell her or Willa was going to faint.

"Okay, so you know I moved out of my family's house six months ago."

I had already lived with Maisie during the semester, but my mother insisted I come back once I graduated. I had no direction and felt lost, so I gave in, thinking now that I had had a taste of freedom, I could handle her emotional manipulation. I moved out again two weeks later and she had been trying to guilt me into moving back home ever since, the final move her misguided kidnapping attempt.

"My mother finally lost her patience and wanted me to move back home," I continued explaining how I got myself into my current predicament.

"Back up the truck, is this why you got attacked? Nora said it was a burglary. You dirty liars. You lied to me and told me some lame-ass story about a robbery."

"I didn't want you to worry."

"Didn't want me to worry? I was already worried and now you're telling me that your mother was trying to kidnap you?" her voice was in a high pitch and the yelling would soon follow.

"Not exactly. She just used someone else to persuade me to come home. No kidnapping happened," I tried to calm her down.

"Only because Mason and Landon were there," she wheezed, her voice sounding like she'd been sucking on some helium.

"This is not even the main part of the story. It's just so you understand why I did what I did."

"Not the main part? Are you trying to kill me? How is you getting kidnapped not the main part? Get on with it or I'm going to pass out."

"Just remember to take deep breaths. At least until I've told you everything."

I compressed the whole shitty tale down into three minutes and finished with, "anyway, so in the end, I agreed to marry David."

Whew, I felt better finally having told someone. And it didn't sound so bad when I said it out loud. Just a little crazy. But not like there was no coming back from it crazy.

"You got engaged without me? And to a guy who is

friends with your mother?" Willa yelled and then there was a crashing sound. I guess she dropped the phone.

"Stella? It's Jameson. We'll call you back in a few minutes. Don't do anything else that seemed like a good idea at the time but will come back and bite you in the ass. Just sit down somewhere until Willa stops hyperventilating and I can get her back on the phone."

He hung up, and I fell back on the bed with a groan. Great, that couldn't have gone any worse. David wasn't so bad. Mostly.

My phone rang again five minutes later. I picked it up from where I had flung it on the bed next to me and sat up.

"It's not as bad as it sounds," I said before Willa could get a word out.

"I agree. It's worse," she said and released a very long and drawn-out sigh. "But we can get you out of this. Send me the contract, and I'll get Jameson's lawyer to look it over."

"I'm not going to send you the contract because I have no intention of getting out of this. I gave my word and signature and that means something to me. And besides, why not go through with it? I have nothing else going for me except my last name. I have no job, no future, and I'm petrified of making the same mistakes over and over again. It's an endless loop with my mother and this is the only way of getting myself out of it. It's a good idea, Willa. Please don't be mad, it's not like he popped the question and you missed it. This is a contract, not a romantic proposal. We talked about it, came to an agreement, he gave me a ring."

A look at my hand confirmed that the ring was still as obnoxious and in-your-face as it had been when David gave it to me when we got to his house. He didn't waste any time making things official. Not sure where he got the ring from on such short notice, but since I didn't care what it looked like, I didn't care where it came from.

"You're petrified?" Willa whispered.

Fuck me and my big mouth. *Too much honesty, Stella.*

"I can't go back to the person I was when I was living with her," I said, my voice wavering. This was harder than I thought it would be.

"Estrella, why didn't you talk to me?" Willa's voice was breaking on the last word, and I felt tears pooling in my eyes.

"I'm sorry, Wills, I just couldn't. And this is not something that I want to talk to you about on the phone. Or with Jameson in the room. No offense, Jameson."

"None taken, honey," Jameson's deep, rumbly voice answered.

"I'm coming home," Willa declared, her voice still wavering.

"No, you're not. You still have a few weeks left, and I would feel incredibly guilty if you came home early because of me. Please don't. I'm fine. Things are fine. We'll talk when you get back. At the time that you're supposed to come back."

"I don't like it. We are so not done talking about this."

I suppressed the tears from escaping. "I know. And we will talk about it. Just not now. Because now I have to go downstairs and figure out how I'm going to pretend to be happily engaged to David."

"I love you. Always."

"And I love you. Always. Now go and do something fun," I said, my voice wavering.

We hung up and I swallowed a few times, trying to dislodge the lump in my throat.

I sent another message to Maisie, hoping she would

answer. Usually, her phone was attached to her hand. Not answering my messages was very unlike her.

It was time to sort out how this arrangement was going to work, and I went downstairs in search of David. He was in his office, sitting behind his large desk, staring at something on his computer screen.

He looked up when he heard me come in. "All settled in?"

"Getting there. What are you up to?" I cringed at the false cheer in my voice. I sure was dreadful at small talk.

"I'm just writing your mother's victory speech."

"Isn't that a bit premature?"

"Not at all. She's going to win the election."

Okay, so I guess being a megalomaniac was contagious. He must have already spent too much time with my mother and convinced himself he was infallible.

"Right, so should we talk about how this is going to work?" I waved a hand around, not sure what I was pointing at.

"I already wrote down some guidelines," David said and grabbed a piece of paper off his desk and held it out to me. I walked over and took it, afraid of what I was going to read. *What had I gotten myself into?*

If I thought it was going to be bad, it was worse.

1. Never disagree with me in public.
2. Always smile when there is a chance someone could take a photo of you.
3. Only wear new clothes, never wear last season's fashion and never the same thing more than once.
4. Join the committee of a charity of your choosing.
5. Lighten your hair—my assistant made you an appointment for tomorrow.

6. Don't let your skin tan.
7. Visit the spa every week—my assistant made you a regular appointment.
8. Only drive the cars I buy for you, and give yours back to your mother. I take care of you from now on.
9. Always be available for public appearances.

"Are you serious?" I asked, not sure I was reading this correctly. Was he insane?

"You may add points to the list, after I've approved them, of course. But that should be enough to get us started."

He was serious. And he didn't even look like he understood why this list might offend me. Or why I might not want to agree to any of the points he'd so kindly laid out for me.

I crumpled up the piece of paper and threw it on the floor. "I'm not agreeing to any of those points. I will be your wife—in name only. No way am I going to turn into your political puppet. Now if you'll excuse me, I have suitcases to unpack."

He followed me upstairs. "You don't agree with the list? That's fine. We can make amendments. But remember you signed a contract, which clearly states that this is going to be a five-year commitment. And that for all intents and purposes, it has to look real. And you know as well as I do that a politician's wife needs to do all these things and more."

I closed my eyes and hung my head. He was right. But that didn't mean I liked it. "We can talk about it later. I just need to get my head around this."

"Fine. But you can't pick and choose what you like

from this arrangement. You made a commitment and need to honor it."

"I get it, okay. Just let me come to terms with it first."

He left me in peace after I closed the door in his face. I half-heartedly unpacked one suitcase but gave up when my hands started shaking from holding back my emotions that tried to bubble to the surface.

I guess I'd royally screwed myself over, going from one controlling home to another. I was a new kind of idiot if I thought I could finally have my freedom. David might be the lesser of two evils, but the next five years were going to be long.

17

"You should try talking to Mason again. He acts before he thinks. I'm sure he regrets firing you," Willa said. I was on the phone with her for the third time today. I'd been staying with David for almost a week and talked to Willa every day.

First, she tried to reason with me and insisted I send her the contract I signed. After I adamantly refused, she tried to talk me into moving back to her apartment. But since me living with David was the only way I didn't have to move back home, it wasn't an option. Not that I told her that part.

"I can't go back to work, Wills. Things were bad when I left," I said and leaned against the kitchen counter, closing my eyes. The stark white cabinets were hurting my eyes.

"Since when are you such a chicken?"

Willa made a clucking sound and I looked up at the ceiling, praying for patience. I didn't get a chance to comment on her impression of a chicken before she started imitating a rooster and was cock-a-doodle-dooing.

"What in the world are you doing?" I asked when the last note of her rooster noises rang out.

"Sorry, couldn't help myself. Any good clucking needs to end in a serious cock-a-doodle-doo."

"It's not gonna work," I tried again.

"All the guys called me. And they promised to have your back and keep Mason far away. So, you have nothing to worry about. It will be fine. And you only have two more weeks until I'm back," she pleaded.

"They called you?"

"Sure did. And they are totally on your side. They said that Mason has been the biggest asshole ever since you left. And Landon is on office duty, which means all the appointments will be booked in wrong. He also doesn't like to use a computer and I expect there to be a lot of sticky notes all over the office."

My heart felt heavy and none of the breaths I took seemed to be getting enough air into my lungs. But going back just wasn't an option. "I really can't, Wills. I'm so sorry to leave you guys hanging like that after everything you've done for me."

"Don't you dare apologize when it's not your fault you're not working there anymore. I'm still going to have a word with Mason though. Nobody treats my friend like that."

"He kind of had a point. I did get engaged to someone else while I was with him."

Not that we'd ever defined our short-lived relationship. But I could see how he would think of my engagement as a betrayal even though I didn't know about it until it happened.

I took another sip of my coffee, feeling more lost than I had after leaving home for the first time.

Things with David weren't going well either. He insisted on having dinner at a restaurant almost every night. That wouldn't have been so bad if the restaurants weren't all strategically chosen for maximum exposure or a two-hour drive away.

Humptulips wasn't exactly a bustling metropolis and the nearest city was Denver. The only reason David was back here was the influence and money my mother had. He was ambitious and smart, not letting any opportunities go to waste.

If he could get someone like my mother to back his campaign, he could start campaigning as soon as he got back to D.C. And he was making sure to lay the groundwork. It looked like I was going to get out of Humptulips after all.

I was relieved he usually worked late, so our interactions were kept to a minimum.

"If he'd only let you explain, he'd know that you had no idea what was going to happen. It's not like you deceived him. I'll kick his ass myself once I'm back home," Willa said, being the great friend I knew her to be. One thing I knew for sure, she'd always be in my corner.

"I better go. David is going to be home soon. We're going to some kind of fundraiser, which I still have to get ready for."

Hopefully the cup of coffee I'd just had would keep me awake.

"I'm not done convincing you to go back yet," she warned me.

She wouldn't be able to change my mind, but it would be nice to hear her voice. "I'll talk to you tomorrow."

We hung up and I went back into the guest bedroom I was staying in. David had made hints of me moving into his room. Hints that I'd pointedly ignored. We would never have that sort of relationship.

Especially not when I was still in love with someone

else. Something I'd come to realize over the last few days, spending time on my own. I just wished I'd done things differently.

But now it was too late and I had to make my peace with the decisions I'd made. I just hoped I wouldn't lose parts of myself in the process.

The dress I was supposed to wear tonight was already laid out for me, courtesy of David's housekeeper. His assistant had purchased it, and his housekeeper would make sure I wore it.

His staff was loyal to him. He paid well and wasn't usually too hard to deal with. Seemed like that was reserved for me. I suspected he didn't like it that I refused to be ordered around by him. He wanted control in all things. And even though I didn't argue about much, already too conditioned by years of living with my mother, there were some things I just wouldn't do. Like sleeping in his bed.

And since it wasn't part of the contract, there was nothing he could do about it.

I sprayed and straightened my hair until it was silky. After twisting it into a chignon, I made sure no hair was out of place.

My makeup was next, each brush stroke practiced and sure. After all, my mother had trained me my whole life for this, so I knew what was expected of me.

I pulled the black satin dress on, the fit perfect as I'd come to expect from anything David purchased for me. It fell down to the floor in shimmery waves, the material light.

Despite its color, I had to admit I liked it. Its fitted bodice hugged me like a second skin, the flared skirt swirling around my feet in soft waves.

The shoes were next—black spiked heels of course—and I was ready with a few minutes to spare.

I used the extra time to add a little perfume and earrings, something I didn't do very often. But if nothing else tonight, at least I would feel beautiful.

And after talking to Willa, I felt more positive than I had in a while. Nothing better than talking to a friend to lift you up.

After one last glance in the mirror to make sure no errant strands had escaped, I went downstairs.

David wasn't home yet, but I pulled on my coat, making sure I was ready as soon as he got here. He didn't like waiting and I didn't have the energy for an argument.

He walked in just as I was putting my phone in my silver sequined clutch that matched my dress.

"You're ready. Great. I'll just put on a different suit and we can go," he greeted me and disappeared up the stairs.

I busied myself with tidying the already gleaming kitchen, putting away my empty coffee mug, and wiping away a few crumbs that were left from my dinner.

Since fundraisers liked to serve fancy food that usually came in tiny portions, I always ate beforehand.

David came back a few minutes later, looking like the polished politician that he was in his black suit and bow tie.

If we'd met under different circumstances, I might even have felt an attraction toward him. He was six foot one, lean, and had light brown hair that was trimmed short.

I knew he took good care of his body, running nearly every morning and watching what he ate.

But since I'd already given my heart away, I felt nothing when he took my hand and led me out to his car.

The drive to Denver was silent. I didn't know what to

talk to him about since we had nothing in common. And he had no idea how to talk to me, judging by the few awkward attempts he'd made.

I wondered if I should make more of an effort. After all, I'd agreed to this arrangement. Nobody made me sign the contract. And five years of uncomfortable silence would make the time go a lot slower.

"Did you have a good day at work?" I asked, deciding I could do better than sitting in the car, brooding.

He glanced over at me before answering, clearly taken by surprise. "It was good. We finalized our campaign strategy and got an extra donor."

"That's great," I responded, trying hard to infuse cheer into my voice. "So, you're still on track to start your campaign in a few months?"

"We are. And we'll also be moving to DC sooner rather than later. Your mom is as good as mayor and as soon as it's official, we're out of this backwards place."

Ouch, that was harsh. I happened to love living here. And it immediately got my back up hearing someone talk shit about my home.

"Guess if that's how you feel about living here, it's a good thing we won't be staying for long."

"You'll like my house in D.C. It's bigger than where we are now and is fully staffed."

I guess a housekeeper and gardener didn't make a full staff, in his opinion. I felt like I was talking to the male version of my mother.

Great job, Stella. You went from one gilded cage to another.

Thankfully we made it to the fundraiser shortly after, cutting off any more conversation we could have had.

As soon as we stepped inside, David was busy shaking hands and talking politics. I was content to stay in the background, watching the rich and entitled prance around the room.

Guess I better get used to it since this is what I'd be doing for the next five years. Really great decision you made there, Stella, signing that contract.

18

"Okay, that's it, time for an intervention," Willa announced and walked into David's guest bedroom where I was buried under the covers.

It was Saturday afternoon and I hadn't left the bed in two days. At first, I thought I was hallucinating when I heard Willa's voice, but as soon as she jumped on the bed and pulled the blankets back, I shot up and hugged her. She pulled me close and I was so relieved she was back, she had to pry my arms open to get me to let go of her.

"Someone's happy to see me," she said and hugged me to her side.

"What are you doing here?" I asked, my eyes blurry from sleeping for pretty much the past twenty-four hours. I couldn't look at her, feeling guilty for forgetting that she got back this morning.

"The how isn't important. What's important is that you get your butt out of bed," she said and wrinkled her nose. "And take a shower."

"I'm so happy you're back but don't take this the wrong way when I tell you to get out," I groaned and pulled the covers over my head.

Willa ripped the blankets off me and jumped on the bed. "Now what's it gonna be, missy? Cold shower? Drink? Exercise. Tell me what you need."

"Sleep."

"Except that. And no crying. There is definitely not going to be more of that. If you start crying, I'll be forced to join you and I have makeup on. So don't you dare screw my face up the one time I look presentable."

I looked at her and noticed not only her flawless makeup but evenly curled hair. That was so unlike Willa that I sat up in surprise.

"What's going on? Why are you so dressed up?"

"Nothing's going on. I just wanted to look nice."

Now I got suspicious. "You never dress up."

"It's nothing. Just felt like dressing up."

"You hate dressing up," I pointed out and all my spidey senses were now on high alert.

She fiddled with the hem of her dress and didn't look at me. Okay, now I definitely knew that something was wrong.

"Willa, talk to me."

"I see what you're doing there, young lady. You are trying to distract me from getting your head out of your ass." She got up on the bed and started jumping up and down. "Stop your conniving ways and start getting up."

I huffed but did as I was told. Willa was like a collie with a ball who just kept going back for more, her energy never-ending once she got her mind set on something.

I sighed but got up and made my way to the bathroom. I needed to wake up before I could start to extract information from my best friend.

"Don't forget to use soap. You stink," she called after me when I disappeared inside the bathroom to take a shower.

Twenty minutes later I was dressed and ready to go.

"How about movies and pizza at my place?" she asked.

I nodded and followed her outside. "Sounds like heaven."

Willa grinned at me and skipped to her car. "Meet you at mine?"

"I'll see you there."

Her car was already parked when I pulled up in front of the apartment building. There was no sight of Willa, but no surprise there.

I used my key to get upstairs and stopped when I walked past Nora's door. I kept babysitting for her throughout the week, and thankfully she had finally told Mason that he didn't have to come as well. Not that he would have, seeing as he was doing his best to avoid me.

Willa's door was open and I pushed through it, closing it behind me. Her apartment was a mess already.

"You feel like a romcom or something more violent?" she asked, scrolling through the options.

"Definitely more in the mood for violence. Something bloody if you have it."

"Of course, I do. This is the age of pay-per-view. I have whatever your broken little heart desires. You can wallow in here for days and not run out of anything to watch. I'll order the pizza now. Want ice cream before or after?" she asked.

"Both," I answered and opened the freezer door.

A mountain of frozen meals came flying out, hitting me in the head and chest. "What in the world," I yelped in surprise and blinked at the now empty freezer.

I picked up a carton of ice cream that had tumbled out as well and put the rest back inside the freezer. The meals were all for weight loss, and I frowned. Why the hell would Willa want to lose weight?

"What's with all the frozen meals, Wills?"

She went red and waved me off. "Those are nothing. Nothing at all. I just thought I'd try something new."

Again with the bullshit answers. She was hiding something from me and I wasn't going to stop until she told me what was going on. Her need to see Jameson would eventually be so great that I could get all her secrets out of her. I'd give it three hours of captivity and she would cry uncle. I cracked my knuckles, ready to take her down.

"Can I take a photo with your phone?" I asked, knowing I had to be strategic about it.

"Sure," the naïve little lamb said and handed it over. I put it in my pocket and went to the door, locking it.

"Hey, I thought you wanted to take a photo."

"I don't. Just needed your phone."

She put her hands on her hips and glared at me. "What's going on?"

"Nope," I said and put up my hand. "That's my line. And you are going to tell me what you're hiding from me."

She looked at the floor. "I'm not hiding anything."

"Really, Wills? Because I know for a fact that you are. You are the shittiest liar in the history of lying and I know all your tells."

"I don't have any tells."

I sighed and opened the ice cream container. "Look, this can be over quickly or we can drag it out. The end result will be the same. Just tell me and we can get on with our lives."

I dipped the spoon in the ice cream and sighed when the first bite hit my tongue.

Willa stepped forward, but I hugged the ice cream container to my chest. "No dessert for you until you spill the beans."

Her lower lip popped out and she gave me her best puppy dog eyes. I shook my head at her amateur move.

"Not gonna work on me, missy. I'm not whipped like Jameson."

"Fine. If you want to know, then I'll tell you."

I raised a brow, waiting for her to continue. She took it as enough of an invitation and did.

"Jameson asked me to marry him. We're engaged. I'm dressed up because I was doing a makeup and hair trial today. I'm trying to lose a few pounds, so I can fit into my mom's wedding dress. There it is. Now are you happy?"

I dropped the spoon and barely caught the ice cream container that started to slip out of my hands.

"And you didn't tell me as soon as it happened?" I screeched, launching myself at her and crushing her to me in a breath-stealing embrace, dropping the ice cream after all. "Is this payback for me getting engaged and you not being there?"

She tapped my back and groaned. "Can't breathe."

"Oh, sorry, didn't mean to squeeze so tight. Just got a little excited." I hugged her again, this time without cutting off her air supply. "I'm so happy for you guys. Congratulations. Have you set a date yet?"

She hugged me back and we separated, both smiling wide. "No date yet. Jameson wanted to elope while we were away. But I want a big wedding and my two best friends at my side when I say I do."

"That's great news, Wills. Why didn't you want to tell me?"

I was hurt that she'd left me out of the loop. Even though I hadn't been the best friend to her lately, we still talked almost every day. She should have told me as soon as he got down on one knee. That's what best friends were supposed to do.

"Well, with your not-so-happy engagement to David, I didn't think you wanted to hear about it yet. I was just trying to give you time. Especially after your breakup with Mason. Something you failed to tell me about, by the way."

"Wills, of course I want to know what's going on with you. And celebrate it. I'm so excited you're getting married, and it couldn't be to a better guy."

I picked my spoon and ice cream up from the floor and got a second spoon out of the drawer for Willa. Every time she said she was on a diet, she would make up the extra calories she saved by eating healthy meals with ice cream. We settled on the couch and started eating the ice cream straight out of the container.

"And I didn't break up with Mason. That would mean we were together in the first place."

"That's not what I was told," she said.

"By who?"

"Landon."

I scraped more ice cream out of the container. "Of course, I could have guessed."

"He said that Mason was beside himself after he fired you. And nobody could talk to him for days for fear of losing an appendage."

"I'm so sorry for everything that happened. I tried to explain but didn't do a very good job of it. But I have to think of Nora. And he was so angry, I think at this stage he is ready to move me to another state himself."

"Oh, I think you're wrong," Willa said, looking smug. "He asks Jameson about you every day."

I tried to ignore the spark of hope flaring to life in my chest. I couldn't get my hopes up and instead changed the topic. I would dissect every word Willa had said later tonight when I was wallowing in my bed. "Tell me what you're planning to do for your engagement party."

Willa's face lit up and she put her spoon down, a clear sign that she meant business. We sat down on the couch, both putting our feet on the coffee table.

"Now that you know, I can start telling people. And we want to get married quickly. So, I was thinking of having the engagement party in a week or two?"

I stared at her. "You haven't told anyone yet?"

"Of course not. I wanted to tell you and Maisie first. You are my best friends."

She held out her fist and I bumped it. I felt tears spring to my eyes.

"You are my best friend in the world, you know that, right?"

"And you are mine," Willa responded, blinking rapidly.

We both lost the fight against the tears, and I found my head squashed to Willa's comfortable boobs.

"We need to stage another intervention. This time for Maisie," she said. I mumbled my agreement, not willing to move my head off its comfortable resting place just yet.

"Are you going to help me plan my party?" Willa asked, playing with my hair.

This time I sat up. "What kind of question is that?"

"Good. Then we need to start with the guest list. And I just want something small. Rayna is doing the catering, but I don't know where we should hold it yet. Jameson lives above the garage, my apartment is too small, and there's no way anything decent will be available to book on such short notice."

I chewed my lip, knowing the perfect place. I just wasn't sure if Mason would be happy with me offering up his farm. But this was about my best friend and his brother. "You should have the party at Mason's place. It's beautiful. Lots of space. And he's done a ton of work to it. The house is massive, and the views are amazing. Perfect location for an engagement party."

Willa clapped her hands, sending bits of ice cream flying everywhere. "Brilliant idea, I'll call Jameson now so he can ask."

Willa held out her hand, and I handed her phone back. The call lasted for half of the movie, and I typed out a lot of text messages and deleted them again while she was gone. They were all to Mason, but none of them made it past a draft.

When my phone binged with an incoming message, I nearly dropped it.

MAISIE: Can you pick me up?
Me: Where are you?
Maisie: On the corner of Petal and Stem.
Me: Be there in 5.
Maisie: Just beep your horn when you're there, I'm hiding behind the bushes and can't see the road properly.

"WILLA?" I called and walked to the kitchen.

She came back out of her room where she'd been holed up talking to Jameson. "Gotta go. Love you too," she said into the phone before hanging up.

"Feel like going for a ride? I have to pick up Maisie."

She put on her shoes and grabbed her coat. "Count me in. She's got some explaining to do."

"I can drive," she said.

"All good, I've got it," I responded, holding up my keys.

As with every other drive within the Humptulips town limits, this one was short, and I came to the corner where Maisie was a few minutes after we left Willa's house.

As soon as I honked the horn, Maisie stumbled out of the bushes that covered the side of the road bordering the park. She ran up to us and dived into the back seat.

"Let's go before he notices I'm gone," she said.

"Who's he?" I asked and pulled away from the curb.

"Oliver."

"Was that who you were with this whole time?" Willa asked, ready to start her inquisition.

"That rat bastard tricked me. I thought I knew him, but he is the devil incarnate. Conniving and ruthless."

I was so confused. Were we talking about the same guy?

"Was he over six foot tall, had dark, almost black hair, blue eyes, and talked with a sexy deep voice? Owns a fortune 500 company?" I asked, just to make sure this was the Oliver we had met in the office.

"Yes, that's him. You can add lying bastard and untrustworthy to the description."

"I think we need an explanation, honey," Willa said. "Let's go back to my apartment. We'll have a sleepover."

"I'm in," I said and turned at the next light to go back to her place. Girls' night in sounded like just what we needed right now.

"Sounds good," Maisie sighed, but didn't sound all too happy about it.

Once we made it back to Willa's place, we all changed into pj's that Willa dug out of her closet for us, and we got comfortable. Maisie and I were sprawled out on the couch; Willa was sitting sideways on her armchair, legs dangling over the armrest.

After watching the movie *300* followed by three of the

Alien movies, we all passed out in a tangle of blankets, popcorn, and chocolate. Maisie refused to talk to us about what had happened and we eventually gave up. She'd spill the beans eventually.

I was the first to wake up the next morning, my heart still hurting but my mind clear. I'd also learned a valuable lesson last night. And that was to never fall asleep first.

I felt wrappers braided into my hair, and I was sure I had something drawn on my face as well. I just hoped they hadn't used Sharpie.

After I confirmed I had a giant heart on my forehead, I washed it off—lucky for me they were feeling generous and used lipstick—and pulled Willa's fluffy robe over my pj's.

I heard Lena crying next door and went over. My knock was answered within seconds, and I was met with a tired-looking Nora, who was trying to calm Lena while Luca was holding on to her leg, asking for breakfast.

"If you come in, I might not let you leave again," Nora greeted me and pulled me inside. I stumbled after her and she only let me go once I was standing in her kitchen.

I got cereal down for Luca and lifted him into his chair. "Do you want blueberries, strawberries, or banana with your cereal today? Or all three?" I asked.

"All fee," he yelled and smiled big.

"All righty then, one healthy bowl of cereal coming right up."

I mixed the milk and cereal and added the fruit before I handed it over to him with a spoon.

"Fank you, Esteballa," he said.

"You are very welcome, cuddlewuddle."

He giggled at my nickname for him and shook his head. "That's not my name."

"Oh yeah? What is it then? Pumpkin? Strawberry? Pear?"

"I'm not a pumelkin."

Nora came back in and I held my arms out to a still-crying Lena. Nora didn't hesitate handing her over.

"What's wrong, baby girl?" I asked Lena and started walking around the apartment.

"She's teething, not sleeping, and wants to be cuddled all the time," Nora sighed and poured herself a cup of coffee. "Now I'm cranky, exhausted, and have no patience left. Which is a terrible combination for my parenting skills and keeping my head together at work."

"Why don't you go back to bed? I've got this," I said and winked at Luca who was still busy slurping up his disgustingly healthy breakfast.

"You don't mind?" she asked.

"I don't have to be at work until eight. And it's only six. That means you can get at least another hour. Doesn't take me long to get ready."

Without another word, she turned on her heels and sprinted to her room.

"Do you want to go visit Wills and Maisie?" I asked Luca once he was finished with his breakfast.

"Yes," he cheered and pumped his little fist in the air.

"Let's get dressed and then we can have a playdate next door."

And for the next hour, Maisie, Willa, and I built a kick-ass blanket fort with Luca while Lena slept through most of it.

19

"Where did you get that dress from? Didn't Clare buy you something for tonight?" David asked with a frown on his face.

"She did," I said, not elaborating further. I hated all of his assistant's choices, the conservative wardrobe so far from my style that I hardly recognized myself every time I wore one of the things she bought.

"Then why aren't you wearing it?" he asked, not done questioning my wardrobe for tonight. Which was ridiculous, since we weren't even at one of his dinners. Tonight, there were no connections to be made or people to impress. Willa's engagement party was family and close friends only.

David was only here because he insisted it would look bad if I went on my own. Not sure who exactly would find out if I went by myself, but I had given up trying to understand how his mind worked. I was also tired of arguing, and taking him with me was the easiest way out.

"I can hardly get changed now, can I?" I asked and frowned down at my green cocktail dress. It was fitted and shorter than he liked. It was made of silk and speckled with small white flowers. I adored the design and the way it hugged my body.

David's permanent frown suggested he thought otherwise.

I had my doubts I would survive the next five years without racking up psychologist bills. In the last few weeks, I started to lose myself, turning more and more into the wife that he wanted me to be and less like the person I was.

The plan that only a short while ago seemed like the perfect solution to all my problems had turned into a trap. I had even less freedom now than I did when I was living with the woman who birthed me.

Now I was stuck and had only myself to blame. David frowned at the food laid out on a big table. He crinkled his nose at the lavender that was used as decoration. He scoffed at the beer that was served in bottles.

Where he hated everything about the country theme of the party, I absolutely adored it. If I could have chosen a flower to display, I would have gone with hints of lavender as well. The smell was subtle and the plants added a nice rich color. Not that I would be choosing my own flowers for either my engagement party or wedding. The wedding planner had things in hand and my participation was neither wanted nor required.

"Estrella," Willa yelled from the other side of the garden, waving her arms at me. She started running in my direction, swaying from side to side like a ship lost in a storm, thanks to wearing stiletto heels on grass.

Willa made it over to us and we hugged. "I'm so glad you're here. I need you to come with me. Now," she said and took my hand. "Sorry, David, I need to steal Stella for a little while. Enjoy the food and drinks, there's plenty."

"Willa. Good to see you again," David said and

nodded his chin at her. He didn't even offer a handshake or hug.

Willa didn't seem to care and took my hand, turning away from David.

Before I had a chance to say anything, she dragged me toward the house and through Mason's overgrown yard that had been transformed into the perfect setting for an engagement party.

"The decorations look amazing, Wills."

"I found this amazing wedding planner that Rayna recommended. Her name is Emerson. I'll introduce you if you want. She could do your engagement and wedding as well since she's just over in Butler."

"David already hired a planner. I would have loved to work with Emerson, though."

"It's *your* wedding. You can still change your mind, I'm sure."

"Not likely."

Willa stopped dragging me behind her and turned to face me. "Stella, I'm just going to say this one thing, and then I'll shut up about it. Promise. But you are making the biggest mistake of your life. Don't marry him. You don't love him and you look miserable. When was the last time you remember feeling happy?"

I wanted to tell her that it hadn't been that long, but the truth was, since I'd moved in with David, I'd been miserable. The last time I was happy was when I was with Mason. She read my facial expression correctly and she squeezed my hand.

"You should talk to him."

"I can't," I whispered, my voice betraying me.

She nodded and continued towing me behind her and up the porch steps. "I'll let it go for now but don't think this is over. Now come on, you need to help me get ready. Oh, and you need to change."

What was everyone's problem with what I was wearing? Seriously, it wasn't a bad dress. And this was just an engagement party. On a farm.

I followed her into one of the guest rooms and stumbled when I saw the white dress draped over the bed.

"Willa, what's going on?" I gasped.

"Surprise," she said and held up her arms. "I'm turning our engagement party into a wedding."

"Does Jameson know about this?"

Willa rolled her eyes at me and handed me a dress in a garment bag. "Whose idea do you think this was? Now put that dress on and then help me with mine."

Holy shit, my best friend was getting married today. *I think I'm going to cry. Scrap that, I'm definitely going to cry. Right now. Yup, there they come Tears. What a disaster.*

"Oh no. No, no, no. Don't cry. You'll ruin your makeup. And we don't have time to redo it. Stop. Think angry thoughts." She wrung her hands and started pacing. "Remember that time I ate the last piece of that chocolate cake you bought from Sweet Dreams? Even though you told me not to eat it and I still did? But I was sad and needed something to make me feel better, so I thought since you were my friend you would want me to have it?"

The tears stopped and I frowned instead. "I was pretty mad at you."

"Total overreaction," she said and stopped moving.

"Maybe a little." I swiped under my eyes, the tears no longer spilling. "Okay, I'm good."

I unzipped the garment bag to reveal a sparkly gold dress. The sequins reflected the light, making the dress shimmer. Willa was smiling so big I was afraid it would be permanent.

"Really? This is what you chose for your bridesmaid's dresses?" I asked, holding it up, amazed one garment could so closely resemble a disco ball.

"You knew this was going to happen."

I did know. And I guess it taught me a valuable lesson to not make declarations after I had a few drinks.

"I was drunk when I said that I would only let you get married if I could wear a sparkly gold dress and be your bridesmaid."

"You're my maid of honor. And I know you want to wear that dress, so shut up and put it on."

"I'm your maid of honor?" I stared at her, the tears welling up again.

"No, no, no, no, think of the chocolate cake."

"You're right. Of course. I'll stop." I waved my hand in front of my face, and when that didn't work, I pinched my side. I yelped but thankfully stopped the tears from falling.

I took off my clothes and slipped into the form-fitting dress. A look in the mirror confirmed it. The dress was exactly what I thought it would be. Way over the top for a wedding, especially as a bridesmaid's dress, but I loved the way it hugged my body in all the right places and how the gold sequins reflected the light just right.

Willa looked me up and down and nodded. "Just like I thought. You are a shit friend, after all. Can't even look bad when I make you squeeze into a disco ball. You could have at least tried for my wedding. I'm the bride after all."

I shook my head and blew her a kiss. "We both know I look more Vegas showgirl than elegant bridesmaid. And nobody could upstage you on your own wedding day." I pointed to her wedding dress. "Ready to put this on?"

"Absolutely. I can't believe this day is really happening. I'm so happy, Stella, I could burst. I'm marrying the man of my dreams, and I didn't even have to drug him to get here."

"Is your dad coming?" I asked, hoping that wouldn't destroy the happy bubble she was floating in.

She looked at the floor. "He's back in rehab. But I didn't want to wait to do this and neither did Jameson. Everyone that means something to Jameson and me is here today. And Maisie promised she would show up as well," Willa said and stripped down to her underwear and strapless bra.

"Don't make me cry again," I warned and pulled her wedding dress out of the garment bag. I helped her pull it over her head and tuck it in place. Lacing it up took forever, and I cursed the whole time. But once I was done, I admitted it was worth the sweat because it looked amazing.

The dress was fitted around the bodice and had cap sleeves. Tiny butterflies sown out of beads were all over the skirt. You could only tell what they were if you looked closely. She looked beautiful and so incredibly happy; she was glowing.

"Willa," I gasped. "This dress was made for you."

She blew me a kiss and grinned. "It was my grandma's who passed it on to my mom. Rayna kept it and gave it to me when she found out I got engaged. I got it altered to fit me, but otherwise it's pretty much the same dress."

"This is going to be the perfect wedding. I'm so happy I get to be here with you."

We hugged, and now it was Willa's turn for a few tears. There was a knock on the door and Rayna popped her head in. Her eyes went wide when she saw Willa.

"Oh my God, you look gorgeous."

Willa twirled, then she twirled again for good measure. "It only needed a few alterations."

"They're almost ready for you," Rayna said. She went over to Willa and took her hands. "I'm so proud of you, baby girl."

There was another knock on the door and Maisie's head appeared. "I'm so damn sorry I'm late."

Willa waved her in. "You just made it."

"What is going on?" Maisie asked and did a double take when she saw Willa. "Are you getting married?"

I handed a gaping Maisie the remaining garment bag and she took it without looking, her eyes stuck on Willa.

"Surprise," Willa said and did another little twirl. "Now get dressed so we can get this show on the road."

Maisie stripped out of her clothes and squeezed herself into the gold dress. I had to give her credit for not saying a word or pulling a face when she saw it.

Maisie was a fashion designer and obsessed with matching her outfits down to the last detail. A gold dress would not make it into her top one hundred.

"Okay, girlies, let's do this," Willa said and grabbed her flowers. "Oh, and you're not only my bridesmaids, you are also going to give me away."

Maisie and I hugged Willa, each taking one side and engulfing her completely.

"Are you sure?" I asked.

"Absolutely. Nobody else I'd rather walk me down the aisle," Willa said.

"Okay, Wills. It'll be our honor," Maisie said and we each stood on one side and took her hands.

We led the way downstairs, and Rayna checked if everyone was in place. When she gave us the okay, we all walked outside to where Jameson, his brother, and Landon stood in front of a beautiful arch wrapped in flowers.

My steps faltered when I locked eyes with Mason, but I was quick to regain my senses and continue walking.

We stopped opposite the guys, and I felt Mason's gaze burning into me. Willa's eyes were on Jameson, who was looking at his bride with so much love and devotion it made my knees shake.

If there was ever anyone made for each other, it was those two.

The ceremony was short and sweet. Willa had always talked about having a ten-minute ceremony and a ten-hour celebration. I guess she really meant it.

I couldn't hold back the tears when they said their vows, and I had given up on wiping them away. I had to fix my makeup anyway, no need to draw more attention to what a mess I was and wiping my face.

As soon as they separated from their kiss that was anything but a chaste peck, everyone descended on the happy couple. I stepped back, needing a minute to collect myself. Somehow, I ended up standing next to Mason.

"How have you been?" he asked, his familiar baritone voice flowing over me.

"Good. You?" I answered, sounding anything but good.

"Good."

We continued standing there in awkward silence, looking at everything but each other.

"Excuse me," I said and walked to the bathroom, unable to stand the tension any longer.

I wondered how long it would take for me to get over him. Because the last few weeks hadn't dimmed my feelings at all. If anything, it had amplified them. Seeing him again, and in a suit for crying out loud, made my heart ache with sorrow. What had I done?

I walked into the upstairs bathroom that I used when I was staying at his house and closed the door behind me. It stopped before it could latch shut and was pushed open again.

I stumbled back and there was Mason, his tie partly undone, his hair sticking up as if he had repeatedly run his hands through it. He turned and shut the door and locked it, resting his forehead on the wood. "Damn it, Stella," he rasped.

What could he possibly be mad at me for now? I hadn't talked to him in weeks, and I didn't think there was anything offensive about our short conversation a few minutes ago.

"What are you doing?" I asked, my whole body one tight mess.

"Why can't I get over you?" he groaned and turned around to face me.

I gaped at him when he stalked over and recognized the fire in his eyes. There was no point in backing up now. If Mason wanted to get closer, he would.

And there was no way I would stop him. I'd missed him too much and would take any scraps I could get. Even if it was only a few stolen moments in a bathroom.

He put his arms around me, one on my waist, the other behind my head, sinking into my hair, and crushed me to him. I gasped at the contact. His mouth met mine and I sighed in relief. Finally.

The feel of him ignited a familiar fire inside me. I arched into him, shuddering at the feel of his body on mine.

The kiss ended as abruptly as it started, and I stumbled at the sudden loss of his touch.

"What the hell are you doing to me? I'm not that guy. You're engaged to someone else," Mason said, breathing heavy, looking torn.

He backed up, his hands interlaced at the back of his

head. His beautiful eyes had lost their vibrancy. The lines on his face seemed harsher.

"If this is what love feels like, then I want nothing to do with it," he sighed and left as quickly as he appeared, leaving me standing in the bathroom, swaying on my feet, more confused than ever.

"Stella, are you in there?" David called. The door was closed but not locked, so he knocked and opened it. "Was that Mason coming out of the bathroom?" he asked, face red, hands balled at his sides.

I couldn't even come up with a good excuse, my brain refusing to work after it had been put under another fog. My silence was enough of an answer for him, and he stepped inside and closed the door behind him.

"How many times do I have to tell you to watch yourself in public," he hissed, careful not to yell. "If you insist on having an affair, do it in private. And with someone who doesn't work at a garage. Jesus, Stella, what is wrong with you?"

"Don't talk to me like that," I snapped, my voice loud. I was angry at Mason for just walking out on me. I was even angrier at myself for not having stood up to David before now. I'd let him walk all over me. But it stopped now.

"I'll talk to you however I want to," he said and turned around. "And we're leaving."

I stayed where I was, crossing my arms over my chest. "You can go home, but I'm staying. I'm not leaving my best friend's wedding before the reception has even started."

He left the bathroom, and I didn't care if he drove away. I'd find a lift into town from someone else and just stay at a hotel.

I locked the door and splashed some water on my face.

I fixed my makeup, and once I felt halfway human again, I went back outside.

There was no sign of David anywhere and I sighed in relief. Willa was standing near the dance floor, her front pressed to Jameson's side, looking happier than I'd ever seen her.

I walked over and she threw herself at me when she saw me. "I'm married," she cried, and we hugged and laughed and hugged some more.

"Congratulations. You are the most beautiful bride I've ever seen."

We released each other and I hugged Jameson. "Congratulations, Jameson. I'm so happy for you both. Just don't ever break her heart or I'll have to kill you."

He let go and Willa stepped right back into her spot by his side.

"You don't have to worry about that," he said and pressed a kiss to Willa's lips.

"Good, because my plan doesn't yet include a way to get rid of the body. Still weighing up the options."

He shook his head and grinned. "No wonder you two are friends. Could have been sisters."

"Might be best not to talk about murder in public, don't you think, Stella," David said, suddenly appearing next to me. Guess he hadn't left without me. Shame, really.

I looked at Willa and we both rolled our eyes.

"Won't happen again," I mumbled and searched for the waiter that was carrying the champagne. I spotted him three people over and excused myself. Hopefully David would follow me—better yet, go home—because the last thing Willa needed on her wedding day was a conversation with Mr. Personality.

I grabbed a glass off the tray and drank half of it on the first sip. Damn, Jameson didn't skimp on anything. The food was amazing, the champagne delicious, and the backyard a fairytale come to life.

David had followed me over and was eyeing the glass in my hand. "Don't you think you've had enough to drink for tonight?"

"I plan on drinking a lot more," I said, feeling rebellious. My eyes wandered around the party, hoping he would get the hint and leave me in peace.

I was mid-sip when I saw the busty blonde who'd been to the garage a few times. She was holding on to Mason, her head tilted up at him and her boobs brushed against his arm. He didn't seem to mind and was talking to her.

I inhaled sharply at the pain that squeezed my ribcage at the sight, and the champagne went down the wrong way, causing me to start coughing uncontrollably. I was afraid I was going to spit up my lung if I didn't stop soon.

"Get a hold of yourself," David chastised from beside me.

"Sorry for choking. I'll try not to do it again," I wheezed and continued coughing. What an asshole.

"Stella. Are you okay?"

I turned away from the voice, stupidly hoping that it wasn't Mason, who was now witnessing my coughing fit. Maybe if I ignored him, he would go away and I could pretend this never happened.

"Here, drink some water," Mason said, and a glass appeared in my line of sight.

I grabbed it and chucked the contents down my throat. Thankfully the water helped, and after a few more coughs, I finally stopped.

"Do you always have to make a spectacle?" David complained next to me.

I turned furious eyes on him and he stepped back. At least he wasn't totally stupid. "Do you think I planned this? If I wanted attention, I would get up on stage and sing. Or start dancing."

"I think we've stayed long enough." He took my arm. "Let's go."

"Let her go," Mason said and stepped in front of us.

"Mason, stop," I said. "This isn't your problem."

At this stage I was ready to crawl under my covers and cry myself to sleep. Going back to David's place sounded like a great idea. And the last thing I wanted was to cause a scene at Willa's wedding.

"You're not going with him," Mason said and didn't move.

"This is none of your business," David said, his calm voice betraying his emotions. His hand was digging into my skin, and I didn't think he would just let this go.

"Anything to do with Stella is my business," Mason said.

"I told you not to get involved with him. This is going to blow back on us," David said next to me.

He liked giving me the I-told-you-so speech. This wasn't the first one I'd received and wouldn't be the last.

"Mason, no offense, but he's right. This is none of your business." I looked from Mason to David. "Now let go of my arm. No scene caused and no casualties recorded. Happy endings all around," I said and looked at the blonde that had followed Mason. "Some might be happier than others."

David didn't let go but tried to step around Mason instead. This wasn't going to end well. Mason was all muscle, not an ounce of fat on him. David was all lean runner with not much muscle.

Mason's sense of justice was also strong. I knew he wouldn't just stand back if someone was hurting or being treated like crap.

"I guess you do want to cause a scene then," Mason said before he stepped forward and punched David straight in the face without hesitation.

"What the hell did you do?" I yelled at Mason and kneeled down to check if David was okay. He was sitting on the ground, holding his nose and groaning, while blood was gushing.

"This is all your fault," David said while glaring at me, his voice muffled from holding his nose.

I ignored his comment and helped him up. "Let's go inside, and I'll get you some ice," I said and led him to the back porch.

"Awesome," Willa exclaimed, stumbling over. "Not only did I get married today, but Mason finally found his balls. Happy days."

I groaned, feeling terrible that I was the cause for all this. "I'm so sorry, Willa. I'll get David out of here."

She grinned big and waved me off. "That was awesome. I saw the punch. No warning, just a well-aimed jab. Way to go, big boy," she said and petted Mason's arm.

I kept leading David into the house, Willa, Mason, and the blonde following.

"Where are you going, Mason?" the blonde squeaked. She was running next to us, her steps small due to the tight fit of her dress.

"What's it look like?" Mason asked, sounding exasperated. Served him right for inviting her.

"But afterward, you'll get me a drink, right?" she whined.

"Nope. And you should go back to your date."

I grinned and looked up at a smiling Willa. If I had my hands free, I would've high-fived her.

"This is turning into the wedding of the year, people.

Give me more drama," Willa said and pumped her hand in the air while she led the way into the kitchen.

I pushed David onto a bar stool and took the ice Willa held out.

"I'm going to sue you," David said, glaring at Mason. His voice still sounded nasally, making me grin behind my hand.

"Now, David," Willa said and walked over to where David was perched. "I trust that you will go home like the well-trained politician you are instead of making another scene. Because I'm sure there are a few things Stella could do to make your life uncomfortable."

David just stared at her, but she seemed to be satisfied with what she saw and nodded. "All right, now that that's sorted, I have a wedding to get back to. You kids behave. And David, I hope you will make the right decision tonight."

With a swirl of her skirt, she went back outside, whistling what sounded a lot like the theme song to *MacGyver*.

David took the ice off his nose, and I noticed that the bleeding had stopped. "Stella, get your things," he said and put the ice on the counter and stood up.

"Get out," Mason ground out and stepped in front of me, facing David.

"Stella," David said, his tone louder. "You know what's on the line."

I did know but couldn't get myself to move. Turned out the decision was taken out of my hands when Mason turned around and put his hands on my waist, nudging me backward. I stumbled in the direction he guided me, confused as to what he was doing.

I heard David storm out and then the front door slammed shut.

My eyes wandered back to Mason, admiring his beautiful face, trying to commit it to memory. Who knew when I'd have a chance to see him again after tonight. We stopped moving just when the back of my feet hit the stairs.

"What are you doing?" I asked when he turned me around and led me up the stairs.

"I tried staying away. But turns out you are more than worth it, and I hope I haven't screwed things up too much for you to give us a second chance."

"I signed a contract. I have to go back to David," I said, the words tumbling out of me.

"You're not really engaged to him?"

I sighed in defeat. "Not in the sense that we love each other. It's just a contract, nothing more. And I honestly didn't know what my mom was up to until that night. I never played you or lied to you."

"I'm sorry I didn't listen to you when you tried explaining things to me," Mason said, sounding pained.

We were now in his bedroom and he led me to his bed. I didn't get a chance to debate whether or not I should sit down when he swept me off my feet and laid me on the bed, coming down on top of me.

"What are you doing?" I asked, my body squirming underneath him, the heat already spreading like wildfire.

"Trying to get you to forgive me and give us another chance," he said, his eyes roaming my face. "What else is in the contract, Stella?"

Maybe it was the alcohol or maybe it was the realization that I needed help, but I spilled the beans like we were about to have a cook-off. I fixed my eyes on Mason's right eyebrow, too scared to look at him.

"I signed a contract that said I had to marry David and stay married for five years. If I don't, then I have to leave the state to make sure it's not going to turn into a media circus. And my mom threatened to get Nora evicted if I didn't play along. There is no way I can let that happen. I'll move if it gets me out of the contact, but Nora is drowning. She needs a break. And she is busting her ass for her kids. No way is she going to survive an eviction."

Mason was quiet for so long it gave me a chance to glance at his face. His jaw was ticking and his eyes were focused on me.

"I wish I hadn't just left," he said.

He didn't have to spell out what he meant. I knew he was talking about the night of the announcement of my engagement.

"It's okay, I understand. It was a lot to take in. Still is."

"I should have believed in what we had," he said, his voice a low rumble. "Especially since I'm in love with you."

My body locked up tight and feelings flooded every inch of me.

"I love you too," I murmured.

I wound my arms around him and held him tight, never wanting to let go.

20

Turned out the only thing it took for me to let go was a knock on Mason's door.

"It's my wedding, and you guys have been up here for too long. Get your asses back downstairs or I'll be forced to come inside," Willa yelled, a slight slur to her voice.

There was a shuffle, and then I heard muffled voices before Willa started yelling again. "It's my wedding and I do what I want. And I want Stella by my side for my first dance. Get your skinny ass downstairs, or I'll show everyone the photo of you dancing in a drag show."

Mason buried his head in my neck and his body shook from laughter. I put my hand in his hair, playing with his soft strands. "We should do what she says. It's her wedding after all," I said.

Mason lifted his head. "I want to see that photo. And I guess I can share you for a few hours until she passes out."

I brushed my lips over his and sat up. "Let's do this before I decide the dresser isn't too heavy to push in front of the door."

I dragged myself away from him and to the bathroom to fix my hair and makeup. The mirror confirmed my worst fears: my hair was sticking up every which way and my makeup had moved from where it was supposed to be to everywhere it wasn't.

I cleaned up as best as I could with only mascara and lipstick in my bag. At least my hair was easy to pin back and I had good skin, so I didn't really need foundation anyway.

It took me only five minutes to get myself together again, and when I walked back into the bedroom, Mason was fully dressed and sitting on the bed, tying his shoes.

"Ready?" he asked, looking up.

I nodded, no words forming at how much I loved watching him do something as simple as tying his shoes.

I couldn't stop the big smile from spreading over my face as we walked downstairs hand in hand.

"Finally," Willa greeted us when we stepped back outside. Jameson appeared next to her and put his arms around her.

I smiled at a tipsy Willa who looked happier than I had ever seen her. Maisie joined us, her cheeks flushed and her movements jerky. I guess I had missed out on some drinking.

"Estrella, you're back," she greeted me and opened her arms to hug me, clocking Mason on the jaw in the process.

"Maisie, looks like you're having fun," I said and chuckled when she rained kisses on my cheek.

"I'm having a great time. This is so much fun. Willa, your wedding is magical. Maybe if I rub your belly, some of your magic will rub off on me," Maisie said and turned to Willa and rubbed her belly.

Willa stuck out her midsection for better access. "Rub away. I'm feeling generous since it's my wedding."

Her eyes went soft on the last word and the permanent

smile on her face seemed to grow bigger. "Time to dance, girlies."

She stood back up and Maisie stopped her assault. "Stella, Maisie, you're with me," Willa declared and took both our hands and dragged us to the dance floor. Jameson went up to the DJ and "Wannabe" by the Spice Girls came on.

Willa turned to us. "Okay, it's showtime. We're doing 'the dance.'"

Maisie and I groaned. "That's the most embarrassing thing you could have asked us to do," I said and wished I had time for a few more drinks.

"It's my wedding, and I dance how I want to. If I want you to do the chicken dance, then you'll do the chicken dance," Willa declared and strutted to the middle of the dance floor.

"She's got a point. And at least she isn't making us do the chicken dance," Maisie said and followed her.

"Not yet," I whispered loudly. There wasn't anything I wouldn't do for Willa. Even if it meant embarrassing myself in front of Mason. Because he was the only one besides Will and Maisie whose opinion I cared about. Hopefully he'd still find me attractive after this dance. Because it was anything but sexy.

Willa started doing what could be called a tap dance, if you had a good imagination. We joined in after taking a few big breaths. Our routine was coordinated down to the smallest arm movement, honed by many hijacked study sessions. There were a lot of things you could do when you were trying to procrastinate writing an assignment. Drinking and making up dance moves was our preferred method.

We wiggled, we twirled, we hopped, we dropped down to the floor, and sidestepped until we hit the end of the dance floor. Then we did it all over again. Our grand finale was coming up and we moonwalked to the center of the dance floor again.

Willa ended our performance with a handstand, Maisie and I on each side, holding her legs up with one hand, the other arm pointed up. The puffy skirt of Willa's wedding dress dropped to the ground and her head was buried under a mountain of tulle. It was the perfect ending to the show, flashing panties and all.

There was thunderous applause, and once we helped Willa back upright, we curtsied.

Jameson came over and claimed Willa. "Thanks, ladies. That was quite impressive. Now it's my turn."

Marvin Gaye's "Let's Get It On" came on, and I stood off to the side with Maisie. We watched Jameson skilfully lead Willa around the dance floor. She was anything but an accomplished dancer, but they looked beautiful together, and Jameson managed to coax her into a few turns without her tripping over her own feet.

Mason joined me and hugged my back to his front, swaying us to the music. I didn't think it was possible for me to get to this point, and it didn't feel real. There was so much I had to sort out with David, but for tonight I would just enjoy myself and celebrate my friends getting married.

We drank, we laughed, we danced, and once Jameson herded Willa outside, we all followed to say our goodbyes. There was a Talbot Lago Grand Sport waiting for them, and Jameson stood speechless in front of the classic car while Willa squealed.

"How did you find this?" Jameson asked Willa once he picked his jaw up off the floor.

Willa shook her head and nodded in Mason's direction. "While I would love to take credit for this one, it wasn't me."

Jameson turned to Mason who shrugged. "I knew you always wanted to drive one. Called in a few favors, since it's your wedding and all."

Jameson crushed Mason to him and the brothers embraced. I heard a sniffle and found Mrs. Drake standing next to me, watching with glassy eyes, a tissue in her hand. I had met her earlier and loved her immediately. She was welcoming and easy to talk to, and it was clear she loved her boys, who felt the same about her.

"Wish I'd thought of that," Willa said, putting her arm around her mother-in-law.

The car really was something else. It had been polished to within an inch of its life, making the black paint shine. The sleek body was the height of elegance and style.

Jameson walked around the car with Mason, taking in every detail. Willa was chatting with Mrs. Drake, who was no longer clutching a tissue but instead laughing. My friend had that effect on people.

The guys finished their inspection, and Mason took Willa's place next to his mom. After Willa said goodbye to everyone at least three times and hugged each person just as often, Jameson managed to get her into the car.

We waved them off, and once the car disappeared behind the trees, we went back into the yard.

"You ready to go back upstairs?" Mason asked me after he helped his mom sit down and got her a glass of water.

"You really need to ask?" I tilted my head back to look at all that was him. His tie was loose and his hair dishevelled, since I couldn't help but run my fingers through it all night.

"Let me just tell Maisie that I'm leaving," I said.

"Okay, beautiful. I'll sit with my mom while you chat to your girl."

Mason kissed my cheek and joined his mom while I

searched the party for Maisie. She was easy to find in her dress, and I walked to where she was talking to Landon who was without his date.

"Cream Puffin, you look radiant. Love the new look," Landon greeted me. He put his arm around me and squeezed me to his side. "You look good, all happy and smiling."

I elbowed his side and stepped away. "And you look so much better without the peroxide blonde on your arm."

"She was easy, and that's just how I like them," he said and winked. "But I've come to my senses when she tried hitting on Mason again. Sent her home. You proud of me?"

"So proud," I said and turned to Maisie. "I'm out of here. You need me to get you a lift before I head inside?"

"All good. Landon offered to drive me home."

I eyed Landon, trying to determine if he was in any state to drive. He interpreted my look correctly and held up a bottle of water. "I've only had one beer when I first got here and water since."

I hugged Maisie. "You still owe me an explanation. Call me tomorrow?"

"I will. Promise."

We separated, and Landon pulled me off my feet and spun me around. "See you later, sparkles. Enjoy your night. Glad you guys made up. The garage was becoming a dark and gloomy place."

I waved at them over my shoulder and joined Mason and his mom. "Ready?"

Mason got up and kissed his mom on the cheek. "See you tomorrow. Don't forget to let Darren know when you want to go home. He's in charge of everyone getting back in one piece."

"I will, honey," she said and smiled at me. "It was

lovely to meet you, Stella. I hope I see you at Sunday dinner."

Mason answered for me. "We'll be there. Good night, Mom."

We silently walked back to Mason's room, and I was pressed up against the wall and kissing Mason as soon as the door shut behind us.

The perfect ending to a perfect wedding.

21

"We'll never get the Viper done if you don't stop interrupting," Landon griped and sighed very long and very loud.

I was too busy giving him the finger while kissing Mason to respond. Turned out that Mason was the perfect boyfriend, and I was addicted.

One hurdle we hadn't managed to overcome was my engagement to David. I hadn't been back to his house or spoken to him since Willa's wedding. It was pretty clear that we couldn't continue our engagement, but I hadn't figured out a way to get out of it without hurting Nora.

As Willa suggested, I talked to Jameson's lawyer who told me that the only way out was to leave the state for a few months. And of course, Nora might lose her apartment if my mother was feeling especially vindictive. Which was highly likely.

As a result, I hadn't talked to David yet and officially our engagement still existed. Unofficially, I stayed with Mason and couldn't have been happier, despite not knowing what the future would bring.

I still had no direction on what to do with my life, but

for the first time I was happy. Blissfully, irrevocably happy. And if the smile Mason was giving me was any indication, then he felt the same way. At least I hoped he did.

"Stella, get your butt back in here. We're not done yet," Willa yelled from the open office door. I was helping her sort out the files Landon had messed up. We also had to rebook a lot of appointments that were double booked on the calendar. At least it gave me a few more days of work while I looked for another job.

"I'm coming. Geesh, you'd think she was performing lifesaving surgery, and I'd walked out halfway through," I grumbled and kissed Mason one last time.

"Hold that thought," Mason said and placed a soft kiss at the edge of my lips.

"What thought?" I asked, distracted.

"The first one," he replied and let me go. It took me a few seconds to catch up, but once I did, I smiled at him and said, "You're on. Better finish up early tonight. We apparently have plans."

"I think I just threw up a little," Landon gagged next to us.

I ignored him and went back to the office. Willa was at the computer, typing something into a word document.

"About time you got back in here," she complained but smiled at the same time. "You know what this means, right?"

"No, but I'm sure you'll enlighten me," I responded and sat down on the chair next to her.

"We're going to be sisters! This is so exciting."

"Aren't you getting slightly ahead of yourself?"

I wasn't even officially living with Mason yet. And it was probably a bit too early for a wedding announcement.

We kept working on saving all the data, while

answering phones and scheduling new work. It was almost four when Mason came into the office.

"Hey, gorgeous," he greeted me and plucked me out of the chair and kissed me.

"Hey," I said once he put me down on my feet.

"I like this," Willa said, grinning while pointing at the two of us.

"We're going to head out," Mason said.

Willa waved us off. "Go forth and do your thing. Or each other."

I giggled and Mason shook his head. "Okay, then," Mason said and put his arm around my shoulders. "I want to show you something," he said and kissed the side of my head.

Well, that sounded perfectly ominous. Could be anything from his perfect body to a cake.

We walked out to the parking lot and instead of going to his car, he steered me to where a motorbike was parked. Closer inspection confirmed that it was the bike I'd seen in his barn.

He took one of the helmets off the handle and handed it to me. "You know how to put one of these on?"

I did not. But it couldn't be that hard, so I took it and put it on my head. It fit snugly, and I was fumbling with the straps that felt like they weren't ever going to fit together. Who designed these things? Shouldn't it be easy to put them on?

Mason put his helmet on and closed the straps, the whole thing taking less than three seconds.

"Need some help?" he asked.

"I think the straps are broken," I said but tilted my head back so he could help me.

It took him less than two seconds to fasten it.

"Thanks," I mumbled.

He took the stand off and sat down on the seat, balancing the bike. "Okay, just sit down behind me and put your arms around my middle," he instructed and held out a hand.

I took it and swung my leg up and over. My arms went around him, and I shuffled as close as I could get.

"All you need to know is hold on tight and lean into the corners. Everything else will come naturally," he said and squeezed my hands. I scooted as close as I could, loving the idea of riding a motorcycle with him.

Things only got better once he started the engine and the vibrations of the motor flowed through my body. A girl could get used to this. That was my last coherent thought before we took off and my heart dropped and my eyes went wide.

He drove out of town and into the mountains, the windy road the perfect place to take a ride. I was stiff as a board at first, not leaning into the corners despite Mason's coaxing. He was going slow, but it felt like he was racing at a thousand miles an hour.

After a while of listening to the drone of the motor and watching the trees and hills go past, I finally relaxed. I started blinking again and my heart rate slowed down.

Once I didn't think I was going to die in a glowing ball of fire anymore, I felt like I was flying. It turned into one of the best experiences of my life. No matter what the future would bring, I was ready because I had Mason. He had given me my life back and I would never forget that.

We eventually stopped at a lookout and dismounted. My legs felt like jelly, and I couldn't undo the straps on my helmet. I was sure they were broken.

Mason helped me with both, first taking the helmet off, then leading me to a bench that sat off to the side of the parking lot. I sank onto the seat in relief.

"What do you think?" Mason asked and sat down next to me, the sides of our bodies pressed together. He was constantly touching me whenever I was close enough, and when I was not, he would always seek me out. I wasn't much better, barely able to keep my clothes on when he was around.

"I loved it. When can we do it again?" I asked and leaned into him.

He laughed and kissed my head. I leaned into him and tipped my head back. Our mouths met, the connection as strong as ever, the simple kiss causing my body to break out in goose bumps. His lips were soft and he tasted of the cupcakes I got everyone from Sweet Dreams.

"We can go for a ride whenever you want. And we still have to drive back as well."

"I decree we become a Sunday ride couple," I said.

"You'll get no objections from me. I love that you like riding with me," he said and stared at me with his beautiful eyes. "I have one more thing to show you. Ready to head back?"

"Let's do it," I answered, getting up. I was wondering what he was up to. The ride back was quicker, since Mason went faster than on the way up, not having to wait for me to adjust anymore.

We drove back into town and Mason parked his bike in front of a small house. The street was quiet and there was a park across the road. The house looked well-maintained, the freshly paved driveway leading up to a double garage.

He pulled up to the garage, and after I got off, he did the same, helping me with my helmet again.

"What are we doing here?" I asked, confused. He already had a house, and I wasn't in the market to buy anything.

"Follow me," he said and took my hand. He walked up

to the front door and unlocked it. The inside was freshly renovated, a cozy living room sitting off to the right of the front door, a kitchen just behind it, overlooking the garden.

Mason showed me around, walking from the kitchen back out into the hallway and past two bedrooms. The one-story house was cozy, and all the bedrooms were a great size. The appliances looked brand new, even the laundry had a new washer and dryer.

"This is really nice," I said, still confused. "But why are you showing me this?"

"It's mine. I just finished renovating it."

"What? I didn't know you owned another house."

"I own a few houses in Humptulips. I've been buying and selling them for a while. It's made me some extra cash after I stopped racing cars. But I want to concentrate on the farm for now. That's why I don't mind if I don't sell this for a while."

"Okay," I said, not sure why he was telling me this. He must have heard the hesitancy in my voice and explained.

"It's for Nora. She and the kids can stay here for as long as they want. Luca is full of energy and loves playing outside. He needs a yard to run around in, and there's a playground just across the street."

It finally clicked, and I realized why he was offering this place up. He knew how much I wanted to help Nora. This was his way of helping me with that. I was speechless.

So instead of saying something that would never be adequate, I threw myself into his arms and kissed him. There was a lot of tongue, it was wet, it was messy, but it was one of the best kisses of my life. Which seemed to be the case with most kisses between Mason and me.

We eventually broke apart, breathing heavily. Mason put his forehead to mine and held me close. "I know how important she is to you and how much you were worrying about her and the kids. And those two sticky gremlins have kind of grown on me. It would be nice to see them settled and not having to worry about losing their home."

"You are the best person I know. I love you so much. Thank you for this; it means the world to me," I said and kissed him again. He had just cut the last string that tied me to David.

"Let's go call the lawyer, so he can start getting me out of that contract."

"Yes, let's. And if you still have to leave the state for a while, then we'll deal with it. Together," Mason said, and we went back outside.

I didn't like the idea of having to be away from Mason, but if it bought me my freedom and meant we could finally be together, then I could deal with a few months being separated from him. He was my forever, and I loved him more than I ever thought one person could love another. He was my missing piece, my temptation that I would gladly give in to over and over again.

EPILOGUE

"I still don't know what you did to get my mother to back off," I said, tracing the tattoo on Mason's bare chest. We were in Glendale Springs, North Carolina, staying at a cabin in the woods. It was pure heaven. The small cabin had one room that included a king-size bed, small kitchenette, a couch, and an open fireplace.

We were three weeks into a four-month road trip across the US on Mason's motorbike. I was no longer engaged and we decided to start our trip with the Blue Ridge Parkway.

My ass was sore from riding every day, but my heart was full. Being with Mason like that, doing something we both loved, was everything. We only rode a few hours every day, frequently stopping along the way. It was a slow trip but we had a few months to kill, after all. Not even the shark of a lawyer I had could get me out of not having to leave the state.

Mason suggested a road trip, something he had always wanted to do. Jameson was more than happy to handle things at the garage, especially since he just employed another mechanic; he and Willa also offered to stay at

Mason's house to take care of the animals while we were gone.

"Your mom didn't tell you?" he asked, sounding surprised.

"I haven't spoke to her since I left."

He hugged me close and sighed. "So, there is no chance of you ever forgiving her and going back?"

"None at all. I hope this doesn't make me sound cold, but I don't want to have anything to do with her."

Mason kissed my head. "The day you officially ended your engagement to David was also the day I officially ended your connection to your mother."

I was confused. I had heard nothing of him visiting my mother. I sat up on my elbow and looked at him. "What do you mean?"

"Just promise not to freak out when I tell you. And remember that you love me."

"Nothing could ever change the way I feel about you. Just tell me what you did."

I was starting to get worried. There wasn't much that would stop my mother from interfering. I may have gotten out of the engagement to David, but that didn't mean that I had gotten out of my obligations to my mother.

Mason studied my face and nodded. "Okay. But come back down here first."

I complied and was now lying half on him, our legs tangled together.

"I figured the only way to get you out was to bend the truth a little."

He took my hand and started playing with my fingers. "I really thought you already knew what I did. I hope you know I would never hide anything from you."

I sat up again, deciding the next few words had to be said looking at him. "I know the person you are, and that's a generous, kind, and loving man who would do anything for his family. A man who puts his life on hold just so he can travel around America with me on his motorbike. A man who makes me feel beautiful and cherished every minute of every day. A man I love more than anything. I know that whatever you did came from a good place."

"Just remember this when I tell you what I said to her."

He pulled me back down on his chest, rearranging me so I was now completely lying on top of him. "I told your mother that we were engaged, and that's why you couldn't marry David."

My body went still and my eyes felt like they were going to pop out of my head. "Did you just say that—"

"We got engaged. Correct." His arms tightened around me. "We both know that was the only thing that would force her to let you go."

I wheezed out a breath, unsure how to respond.

Mason took that as his cue to keep going. "Things got a little heated, and I may have also hinted at the possibility of a pregnancy."

My lungs filled with air, and I shot up to kneeling, straddling him. "Are you crazy? Why would you do that? I could make my peace with a fake engagement. But pregnancy?"

"I panicked. She's scary when she's angry. I figured we'd get there eventually. So, I wasn't *really* lying. After all, I didn't specify if you were already pregnant."

I glared at him. "I don't know if I should be mad at you or impressed. But since I haven't heard a word from my mother, it seems your ploy worked."

He ran his hands up my thighs, stopping at my butt and gripping it, pulling me closer. "I vote you go with impressed."

His hands made their way up my back, pulling me down until our faces were almost touching.

"Thank you, it means everything to me that you talked to her," I said, feeling tears well up. He'd done the one thing I'd always wanted. Gotten my mother to back off. Even if he lied to her.

"I would do anything for you. You are the one temptation I can't resist, and I don't plan on ever giving you up."

"I think you should show me just how much of a temptation you think I am. I can barely remember the last time."

And show me he did. He was my missing piece, the holder of my heart, the one I wanted to spend the rest of my life with. I had finally found my place in the world and couldn't wait to see what the future had in store. Because as long as I had Mason by my side, I was ready for anything.

Thank you so much for reading Some Call It Temptation. The series continues with Maisie and Oliver's story. Read on for an excerpt.

If you enjoyed this book, please consider leaving a review. They help other readers discover my stories and are the fuel that keeps authors going.

DON'T FORGET to sign up to my newsletter for news on upcoming books and to receive a newsletter exclusive novella (set in the Sweet Dreams series world).

SOME CALL IT FATE
CHAPTER 1

"This will never happen again," I said and buttoned up my blouse. "I'm serious. We're done."

"Are you as done as you were last time you said you were done or the time before that?"

I cut my eyes to Oliver, who was still in bed, sitting up against the cushions, the sheet pooled around his lap. I debated if it was a good idea to pull the sheet down since I wouldn't mind one last glance at the goods. After all, this would be the last time we'd see each other without our clothes on. I meant it this time. This was it.

"I have to go," I said and brushed my hair back, looking for my purse. I spotted it under the table where it landed when I threw it into the room as soon as we entered. Like so many times before, the moment the door closed behind us, we came together like addicts, wasting no time to get our next fix. And that was all this was—an unhealthy addiction that needed to stop.

The rustle of the bedsheets told me Oliver was getting up. I had to hustle to get out of there, because if he came too close, I would fall back into his orbit and do something I'd regret later.

A warm hand landed on my back, and I tensed, purse forgotten. "Wh-What are you doing?" I stuttered and looked over my shoulder at what must have been one of the most perfect men I had ever seen.

At over six feet, with dark, almost black hair, sapphire blue eyes, and a deep voice that I could listen to forever, he was sex personified. We had been seeing each other nearly every day for the last six months. I insisted it was all casual; he was sure we were more than that. But his time in Humptulips was temporary, hence why he had been living at a bed-and-breakfast since he arrived.

Even though I knew better, I let myself get sucked into another relationship that had no future. Something I now had to pay for. Because despite my declarations that this would never be more than a casual hookup, I had developed feelings. Ooey, gooey, disgusting feelings that made me dissolve into a puddle of want every time I looked at his beautiful angular face with his high cheekbones and that dimple in his left cheek.

And Maisie Slater didn't do feelings anymore. Not after getting her heart smashed and pulverized not once but twice in her short life. Also, Maisie needed to stop talking about herself in third person.

Before I made another mistake and fell back into bed with him, I turned and ran as fast as my untrained short legs would take me. The door was unlocked, since we didn't have time to lock it when we came inside. Guess that happened when you were too busy ripping your clothes off and kissing and sucking every inch of skin you could get your mouth on.

But I wasn't going there. Nope. Instead, I concentrated on running in my boots with impossibly high heels. But they looked kickass, and I got them from one of my friends from college, Lisa, who was trying out a new line. It paid to have trendy friends in even trendier places. Unless you needed to run away.

I burst out onto the road and swiveled my head from left to right, resembling a scene from the *Exorcist*. Which would be the least likely path Oliver would think I'd take? I saw the sign for Drake's Garage and pushed my legs to go as fast as they could carry me. Which wasn't quick, though better than walking.

The garage was a bit out of town, and so was the bed-and-breakfast Oliver was staying at. For once in my life, luck seemed to be on my side, because one of my best friends, Stella, was working at the garage for a few weeks. Oliver hadn't met any of my friends so I thought he wouldn't know to look for me there. I burst into her office, shouting, "Stella, you have to hide me. Now."

And since she was one of the good ones, she pushed me under her desk and put the chair in front of me, asking no questions. I was small enough to fit without a problem and let out a deep breath.

"I'll explain later," I said while curling up into a ball. This was definitely one of the low points in my life. *Damn you, Oliver.*

The huge desk was enclosed on three sides, which made it an excellent place to hide. I heard Stella's voice above me, keeping up the charade. "Sorry, we're closed."

"Where is Maisie?" Oliver's deep voice sounded from the other side of the desk.

"I don't know. Have you tried the bakery three streets over?" she asked, never missing a beat. Damn, she was good.

"I saw her run in here."

"Can I help you?" another voice asked. It sounded like Mason, but I wasn't sure.

"Hi, I'm Oliver Thorpe. I'm looking for Maisie."

"As in Thorpe Holdings?" maybe-Mason asked. There was awe in his voice. Why was there awe in his voice? Did he know something I didn't?

"The very one," Oliver responded.

"Nice to meet you. If you want to book your car, Stella is happy to do that for you."

"No she's not. Stella needs to close the office and go home," my bestest of the best friends said.

"Thanks, but I don't need any work done on my car. Only bought it a few weeks ago," Oliver said. "I really need to talk to Maisie though."

"Her name is Stella," maybe-Mason said.

"Nice to meet you, Stella. Now can I talk to Maisie?"

I was getting uncomfortable but was too afraid to move. It was humiliating enough being a grown-ass woman who was hiding under a desk.

The muffled conversation continued, and then Stella said, "Not sure when I saw her last, sorry."

Gotta love her commitment. But at this stage, we both knew the jig was up. Yet here I was, still crammed under her desk.

"Look, I saw her run in here. I know she's hiding so she won't have to talk to me," Oliver said, and I heard something land on the desk. "Can you make sure she gets this?"

I heard Stella say, "Sure. No problem." At least the torture was almost over.

"Thanks. And tell her I'll see her at my sister's birthday party," Oliver said.

After a few more seconds, the front door closed, and Stella leaned down and pushed the chair out of the way, grinning.

"Who the hell was that?" she asked.

I struggled out from underneath the desk and avoided eye contact. "Just some guy."

"Liar. I want to know what the hell is going on," she said, knowing full well there was more to the story.

"Nothing is going on. He thinks he has some sort of claim on me, but he doesn't. Now, can we forget this embarrassing scene ever happened? And promise not to tell anyone."

Stella grinned and pointed behind me. "If you can convince him to keep quiet, you might have a shot."

I jumped when I saw one of the owners of Drake's Garage. I had already forgotten about the third voice and had hoped against hope that it wasn't Mason. "What are you doing in the office? Don't you have your mechanic thing to do?"

Mason narrowed his eyes at me. "It's my garage, and I can be wherever I want to be. And right now, I want to be in the office because seems to me like Stella forgot she works here. Not sure why you're here either."

I stood up straight, not letting him intimidate me. "I'm visiting Stella to make sure you haven't made her quit yet."

"Still working on it."

"Lucky I need the money," Stella grumbled.

"Have you finally been cut off?" Mason asked.

"Why don't you get back to whatever it was you were doing before you came in here?" she asked, her face pinched.

"Gladly," Mason drawled and left.

As soon as the door closed behind him with a loud bang, Stella's shoulders slumped forward and she exhaled loudly.

"Seems like I'm not the only one keeping secrets," I said.

"Ha, so you admit to keeping Mr. GQ a secret. I knew it."

I grinned at Stella and took her hand. "Come on, seems like we have a lot of catching up to do."

"Should we head to The Grill?" she asked.

"What kind of question is that?" I answered and grinned.

Stella laughed and squeezed my hand. "I missed you these last few weeks. No more overseas internships."

"I missed you too, Estrella, and there are no more trips in my future. Europe is overrated anyway. Now, I hope you have your car here, because Lincoln dropped me off."

Stella's dad was Colombian and died when she was little. Her mom erased any traces of him from their lives, which included speaking Spanish. Since Stella had already lost so much, Willa and I tried to find little ways of using Spanish words here and there. The nickname Estrella stuck after the first time Willa called her that, and now we all used it.

Lincoln dropped me off at my store this morning on his way into town. I was supposed to catch a ride back to the house with him, but Oliver picked me up from the store, and here I was without a car.

Lincoln was one of my three roommates and a computer nerd. He also owned the house we all lived in. Our relationship had turned from roommates to friends, and I liked hanging out with him. He was a friendly guy who went above and beyond for his friends. There used to be four of us in the house, but Des, our fourth roommate, got a job in New York and moved a while ago.

"Lincoln, huh?" Stella teased me on our way out.

I groaned. "Don't start."

Getting a place where I not only had my own bathroom but also enough room to never see my roommates if I didn't want to was divine intervention.

Lincoln bought the house—if you could call a six-bedroom, seven-bathroom mansion a house—a few years ago and renovated it. He said it was too big for just him, and now there were four of us living there.

"How did you manage to keep your car?" I asked and got into the passenger seat. Things with her mom had been tense, but ever since Stella left home, it was war. Her mom had cut her off from all her accounts, canceled her credit cards, and blacklisted her from all businesses so she couldn't get a job anywhere. Well, except at Drake's Garage. And that was only thanks to Willa, who I knew convinced her boyfriend, Jameson—Mason's brother—to let her work there while they were traveling.

"It was in my name, so my mother couldn't really take it from me. I'll have to sell it though, if I don't get a job soon."

"Honey, you've got a job."

"You know what I mean. A job that won't end in a few weeks."

She had a point. But at least that would give her time to figure out what she wanted to do.

"Are you still staying at Willa's?" I asked.

Stella nodded. "She's at Jameson's most of the time, so she's happy she doesn't have to pay full rent. But I have to find something soon."

We made it to The Grill and hid in a booth toward the back. Neither of us was in the mood for small talk. And since we had both lived here our whole lives—Stella out on a farm and I in a crazy hippie household—we knew pretty much everyone, and everyone knew us.

"Tell me what's going on with Oliver," she said.

"What the hell happened with Mason?" I asked at the same time.

I wasn't ready to talk about Oliver and was way too curious to find out what the hell was going on with her and Mason. I knew him as an easygoing guy, but he was more fire-spitting dragon when I saw him at the garage. At least Stella knew she had to give me something before I started talking.

"Fine. I'll go first. Not that there's much to explain. It's simple really. Mason hates me. I hate Mason. We make each other's lives miserable whenever we run into each other. He thinks I'm a spoiled brat, and I think he has a chip on his shoulder the size of the Rocky Mountains. We only have to put up with each other while I work at the garage, so hopefully there won't be any casualties."

I laughed, and she narrowed her eyes at me. "Hey, stop that. I wasn't finished. I had a lot more to complain about."

I just bet she did. But I also knew the way Mason had looked at her at the garage was not the look of hate. More like lust. Things were about to get interesting.

And since I had put a stop to my romantic life, I could just live vicariously through Stella. "Oh, Estrella, there is no way that guy hates you. And besides, he's one of the nicest guys I've ever met. No way would he be mean to you. You sure you're not overreacting?"

"Don't even go there. This is not a case of pulling someone's pigtails because you like them. He is making my life miserable. And I'm beginning to think he has a point when he calls me princess. I did grow up in a mansion and never wanted for anything."

That stopped my amusement in its tracks. "Stop. I know you. You are a good person and you work hard. You don't expect handouts. It doesn't matter where you come from. What matters is what you do with your life."

I knew how much it hurt Stella when people thought of her as spoiled. She never talked about it much, but from the few things she had told us about her family, I knew she had it tough.

She avoided my eyes, but at least she hadn't shut down yet like so many times in the past when the topic came up. "I know. It's just hard not to feel like a failure. Especially when the only things I own are my clothes and a car."

"So you're just like a lot of other college grads out there. Don't put yourself down like that." And I couldn't really say I was in a much better position.

"Thanks, Maisie," she said and looked at me. "You know I love you, right?"

"Of course you do. Why wouldn't you? I'm pretty awesome. Now let's order some food, because I'm starving, and I already waved Leslie off twice when she tried to take our order. If I do it a third time, she won't come back."

At least she didn't push me about Oliver, and I stole some of her food while she wasn't looking. The night wasn't a complete write-off.

Get Some Call It Fate now

OTHER BOOKS BY SARAH PEIS

Sweet Dreams Series

Some Call It Love (#1)

Some Call It Temptation (#2)

Kismet (#2.5) - exclusive to newsletter subscribers

Some Call It Fate (#3)

Worship (#3.5) - only available in Sweet Dreams Box Set Part Two

Some Call It Devotion (#4)

Glamour (#4.5)

Some Call It Attraction (#5)

Spark (#5.5) – only available in Sweet Dreams Box Set Part Two

Sweet Dreams Box Set Part One

Sweet Dreams Box Set Part Two

Standalones

Adult Supervision Required

Contents May Catch Fire

ABOUT THE AUTHOR

I love the written word in all forms and shapes and if I'm not glued to a book, I'm attempting to write one. I'm a frequent blonde moment sufferer and still haven't figured out how to adult. Lucky google always has an answer, so I don't have to.

I live in Melbourne, Victoria, with my two kids, the holder of my heart and two fur babies. If you want to accompany me on my path to enlightenment, check out my publications or get in touch, I would love to hear from you!

WHERE YOU CAN FIND ME

Join my Blonde Moment Support Group (all hair colours welcome!) on Facebook to talk about blonde moments, parenting fails and of course books.

Facebook
Instagram
Pinterest
www.sarahpeis.com

THANK YOU

Thank you for reading this far,
   A legend is what you are.

   There are so many people to thank,
   But when I get to this part I usually (still) draw a blank.

   Let's start with the beautiful Natasha who helped me once again to make this book the best it can be,
   seeing your suggestions always fills me with glee.

   Ginna, I'll be forever grateful for your amazeballs support, you are simply the best,
   your friendship makes me feel blessed.

   Robyn, there aren't enough words to tell you how much I adore you,
   One day we have to get a matching tattoo.

   To my friends and family who support me in all that I do,
   I f*ing love you!

Becky and Virginia from Hot Tree Editing deserve a special mention at this stage,
Their knowledge and insight brought perfection to each page.

Thank you to the wonderful Ben for creating a kick-ass cover design,
You really make my book shine!

My beautiful mom who reads all my books deserves a special mention at this stage,
She's never afraid to turn the page.

Sim – I could never have done this without you, you are the love of my life,
I'm so proud to be your wife.

Made in the USA
Columbia, SC
04 April 2024